Divided Heart

Book Nine of the Hayle Coven Novels

patti Larsen

Also by

PATTI LARSEN

The Hunted Series

The Hayle Coven Novels

Blood and Gold Trilogy

The Clone Chronicles

The Diamond City Trilogy

The First Plane Trilogy

The Lychos Cycle

The Hayle Coven Destinies

and much, much more.

Find your new favorite author at

pattilarsen.com

Sign up for new releases

bit.ly/pattilarsenemail

I grunted from the weight of the suitcase as I heaved it out of the back of the van. What had I packed again? I didn't remember it being this heavy when I loaded it into the twins' car only seven hours ago.

Seven long and painful hours. I forced a smile as Esther and Estelle stepped up onto the curb, matching prim skirts and twin sets as much their uniform as their very comfortable looking shoes.

They didn't smile back, but through my connection to them from the family magic, I was sure their flat expressions had nothing to do with how they felt about me.

Well. Pretty sure.

Charlotte didn't say a word as she popped out the handle at the top of the suitcase before standing just behind me, waiting. The weregirl's insistence on joining me as my bodyguard hadn't ended with me leaving for college. Quite the opposite. Here I was, first year at Harvard, and I had extra baggage outside my clothes and personal items.

Story of my life.

I kind of felt bad for Charlotte. She'd left all of her own people back in Wilding Springs, even given up looking for her father, Raoul, just to protect me. Out of some misguided honor thing I really didn't understand. Or appreciate, to be honest. This year was going to be new and hopefully all kinds of awesome. I wasn't sure how having a cold, blonde shadow following me everywhere was going to be conducive to fitting in with the rest of the student body.

I focused on the twins, keeping my smile in place as I spoke. "Thank you so much for the drive." The painful, slow, well-below-the-speed-limit drive with two hard-core witches who didn't spend much time in the real world. Why Mom chose them to bring me to school I had no idea. It would have been a whole lot easier if she'd just let me ride the veil. Faster, too. My connection to the demon plane made moving from place to place across the slippery barrier between Demonicon and here super simple.

But I guess using magic for that kind of thing on campus was frowned upon. Stupid rule.

"It was our pleasure." I still couldn't tell them apart with any accuracy, but I guessed it was Esther who spoke. "Considering Miriam was unavailable at the last minute."

Ah yes. Mom. Nothing like thinking about her to put a damper on my pre-college mix of nerves and excitement. Once the leader of my coven, now the grand pooh-bah of the North American Witches Council. Things had changed a lot since Mom left Wilding Springs and the coven to the co-leadership of Gram and I so she could rule the world. Stuff like reliability. Availability. She'd broken so many promises in the few short months since she'd taken over as Council Leader after almost being burned at the stake by that same Council, I didn't bother asking her for anything anymore.

The trip to school by car had been her idea, though, in my defense. *It'll be fun*, she sent in a three-way conversation with me and my sister Meira. *We'll come get you, make a day of the drive.*

I hadn't said anything, though Meira seemed excited. I wondered how my little sister was doing here at Harvard all by herself, a summer spent attending private witch camp and now school, also housed on campus. Well, I guess she had Sassafras. And Dad, when he was able to visit. I found I missed my family even though I stood there just outside Johnson Gate, only steps from seeing them all again.

As much as I was annoyed with my mother? I was at college.

Wicked.

"The Council comes first." I impressed myself. No bitterness. Good for me.

Estelle—yeah, okay, guessing again—glanced at her sister. "I'm certain the situation which kept her from you was important."

There wasn't any judgment in her voice, so at least neither of them though I was being a whiny baby. Not like I really cared, but I was their leader, after all. Mostly. Half. Fine, Gram was really leader. But I'd learned a lot from her this past summer, things I'd never considered to be important. The subtle way she manipulated people was a work of art to behold and left me a little breathless at times, especially when she, without the use of magic outside her own personality and experience, managed to convince whoever it was she talked to it was their idea to give her what she wanted.

Awesome. And a little scary. I'd caught myself doing it on occasion and sucked at it. Didn't help my weak attempts always made Gram laugh.

I missed her all of a sudden, with an emptiness in my heart I wished I could fill by hugging her one more time. Yes, she was always with me, in the back of my mind. But physically she was back home, holding down the fort so I could go to college.

Mind you, she'd want me to continue to act like a coven leader. Which meant even though I wasn't the real hands at the helm of the Hayle family, I still had to put up a good appearance.

Esther hesitated before bobbing a little curtsy, her sister mimicking her perfectly. Before I could do or say anything, the both approached and took one of my hands in each of theirs.

We'll miss you. Their doubled voice echoed in my head, the power behind their connection fed by the dual nature of their abilities. While I was accustomed to them, the feeling of them, I wasn't used to their kindness.

Only a second before I'd been wishing they would just leave already so I could get on with finding out what college was all about, but their joint touch washed my eagerness away. Impulse took over as I leaned forward and hugged them both together, throat tightening as I did, tears springing unexpectedly to my eyes. Silly? Yeah, maybe. But they just reminded me I wasn't in Wilding Springs anymore.

We, too, know what it's like to be away from our coven. I felt their power slide down the connection between us. *The coven, your family, is with you always.*

I sent my own surge of magic, grateful suddenly it was the two of them standing there with me at that moment.

"Drive safe." I backed away, almost tripping over the backpack and second suitcase I'd already unloaded. The twins waved and climbed into their mint green minivan as though they were some perfectly synchronized team. Moving in perfect unison, they slid on their seat belts before Estelle—had to be Estelle—fired up the engine and drove off.

I was not going to cry. Not. I wasn't ten any more, being shipped off to wretched witch camp for the summer. With a start I realized that was the last and only time I'd been away from home for longer than a weekend, and even that I'd only done once with my best friend Alison.

Alison. I couldn't think about her. As I bent to heft my backpack over my shoulder and trudge past the ornate gate onto the property, sadness took over what was left of the excitement I'd felt. The ghostly echo of my friend had popped up now and then over the summer, but only for an instant and never long enough for me to convince her to pass over.

At the time, I didn't need Gram's disapproving glares to tell me what I already knew—Alison had to be dealt with. Would she follow me to school? I felt the tingle of magic as I passed onto the main property of the college and wondered. The oldest part of the school protected with magic was known as Harvard Yard, and had been since John Harvard, himself a member of the now-disbanded Harvard coven used his power and that of his family to ensure witches would always be safe here. It meant no foreign magic was permitted to pass. And though I'd mentioned the fact to Mom, worrying about being a witch/demon/Sidhe princess carrying a vampire virus in a gem around my neck, she assured me she'd cleared me to enter.

It wasn't until Charlotte and I passed over the wards I realized Mom could just as easily have let it slip her mind.

Good thing she hadn't forgotten everything.

My sense of homesickness faded as I entered the grassy Yard, taken over by a fluttering of very active butterflies in the pit of my stomach, a smile pulling my lips back as the extra bounce I'd been experiencing returned to my step. College! The place was stunning and I found myself rubber-necking as I passed under the huge trees towering over the freshmen dorms, red brick mingling with green and the blue of the sky. I dodged a pack of eager new students weighted down with their own belongings as I reminded myself not only was I starting fresh, the chance to let loose a little and meet some other witches at last, I didn't have to worry about being lonely here. I had Mom, or at least, Mom was around. And Meira. Sassafras. Dad even. Mom had moved his statue to Harvard with her when she'd taken over her duties as Council Leader. And there was always my wereshadow.

Suddenly my life was feeling pretty crowded all over again.

But it was the idea of making friends who were witches that made me the most happy. Finally, I'd be in a position where I could interact with peers, with those who had power too and weren't creeped out by the feeling of it. The only person with magic I really considered a friend was Liam. Thinking of him, the handsome O'Dane Gatekeeper, made me sad all over again. I had to shake myself free of the funk.

If I was going to be waffling around emotionally like this for the entire semester I'd be needing sedation.

Still, it didn't seem fair. He was my only friend who understood me, who knew everything about me. And though I'd only said a tearful, huggy goodbye to him and the black hound Galleytrot that morning, it felt like I'd never see him again.

Jeeze, Syd. Get a grip. You're at *college*.

There was only one person who could distract me from thinking about Liam. And I hadn't seen that certain someone in months. Quaid left shortly after Mom's trial ended, accepting Pender Tremere's offer to attend the apprentice Enforcer program. It made me nervous, him going off like that, even though I knew more than ever how much Quaid loved me. And it wasn't like the program was the be all and end all—lots of witches went, partly to train to join the Enforcers, and partly to gain skills they would need to defend their covens. In fact, if I wasn't in the position I was in, half-leader of my family, it's likely I would have ended up there too.

I'm pretty sure Charlotte knew where my head was, because it wasn't long before she circled and herded me toward a large brick building. Hollis Hall was my new home for the year, freshmen residence to normal and witch students alike. I'd already sent some things on to Mom earlier in the week—hopefully she'd had them delivered to my room. I reached out with my magic, felt the pull of my stuff and knew she had.

Helpful. Unlike the normal frosh, I was able to latch onto the feeling of my things and follow them, now that I'd shaken myself out of my rollercoaster emotional state and back into tingling excitement, toward the big dorm.

Magic open, I could now also feel Mom, just a few brick buildings down. I didn't want to see her just yet, though I missed Meira and Sassafras with a sudden ache that almost made me change my mind. But the front doors of Hollis welcomed me inside and I chose to be a normal student and settle myself first instead.

Another tingle of magic made me turn just before I passed the threshold. Right across the Yard from me was the statue of John Harvard. I'd have to visit later, to touch his left shoe for luck. Behind him was the source of the power drawing my attention. The long, white building housed the university offices, as well as the High Council. Hopefully, outside of my hello to John, I wouldn't have a need to spend any time there.

Staying out of trouble this year, making friends, being a typical college student. Yup, that was me.

With Quaid's last promise he'd see me at school hugged to me, I turned my back on the High Council and entered my new life.

The fourth and fifth floors of Hollis Hall was home to witches alone, warded against normal students. Not that they weren't aware the floors were there, but instead felt no desire to visit. The entire campus was like that, places where the ordinary and the magical existed side-by-side, but never met, at least for the normals.

I peeked inside the room calling my name and found myself pleasantly surprised. Yes, it held two beds. Mom insisted I have a roommate my first year. Something about making connections with other witches. But I was pretty sure she really just didn't want it to look like I was getting special treatment. In all honesty, I should have been housed at Gray Hall, the home of the elite. Not all covens were as wealthy as mine, and not all as powerful. Some had more money, some stronger witches, but it was a rare few that had a combination of the two. And though the thought of being segregated with the rich witches no matter their abilities was kind of horrible, I'd taken a look online at the dorms and amenities and had to suppress a sigh of regret I wouldn't be living there.

But this room wasn't so bad. I looked around as I entered, at the wide common space, the bed next to the door already covered with a homey quilt. The one across from it under a large window almost groaned, piled with my stuff. To the right was an open door, the bathroom, I assumed. On the left was a wardrobe next to my bed. I eyed it with some trepidation, wondering if I'd be able to cram all my clothes inside. Not that I was much of a prissy princess, but a girl had to have variety.

Charlotte rolled my two suitcases to the side of my bed and pushed the handles back inside before dumping the second backpack next to the stack of sheets, comforter and pillows, box of personal items and one smaller suitcase full of clothes already waiting for me.

I turned to the weregirl, feeling suddenly awkward. What was she planning, to sleep at the foot of my bed?

Her hint of a smile told me she knew exactly what I was thinking. "I'm in the single across the hall," she said. "Miriam insisted you have a witch roommate." I could tell from the tone of her voice she disagreed with my mother. Charlotte had no problem sharing her disapproval.

It was one thing I really liked about her. If she said something, she meant it and didn't care who heard her.

"Okay then." I looked around, not sure what to tackle first, eyes drifting to the neatly made bed across from me. "Wonder what she's like."

Charlotte's shrug was so subtle if I didn't know her so well I would have missed it. "A witch," she said.

Helpful. Seriously, I'd heard some horror stories from well-meaning coven members who stopped by over tea during the summer to share with me how terrible their roommate experiences were.

Those conversations always ended with a hand pat, a weak smile and a, "I'm sure it will be different for you, Sydlynn."

Now that I stood here in my new room, the one I'd be calling home for the next nine months, those stories came rushing back.

"What if she's, you know. Weird?" I hugged myself a little while Charlotte watched me with her ice blue eyes. Why did I always get the impression she could see right through me?

"Then you'll get along, I suppose." Charlotte just made a joke. Amazing.

"Thanks a lot." I dropped my arms, did my best to relax.

There wasn't much I could do about it now, anyway. Not when the sounds at the door told me my new roommate just arrived.

I turned slowly, forcing a smile, praying silently she was reasonably stable only to find my tension disappearing in a rush as two familiar faces smiled back at me.

Tallah Hensley stepped forward immediately, the young leader of the Hensley coven hugging me with great enthusiasm. Her sister, Sashenka, hung back while Tallah and I embraced.

"I'm so happy to see you, Syd." Tallah leaned away though her hands still gripped my upper arms, white teeth flashing against her glowing dark skin. "It's been fun talking over the last few months, but I was hoping to run into you here, face-to-face."

We'd done our best to keep connected after Mom's trial was over. I genuinely liked the Hensley sisters, though Tallah was the most open and forward of the pair. I always got the impression Sashenka felt like her sister overshadowed her and hoped her time at college would help her to feel more independent.

I exchanged a quick hug with Sashenka, very happy to see her. "I can't tell you how relieved I am you're my roommate."

Her smile was a little nervous, but Sashenka nodded with enthusiasm. "Tallah requested we be together," she said. "I hope you don't mind?"

"Not even a little." I suddenly felt a whole lot better. This year might end up fantastic after all. I had my first witch friend at college already and I'd only been here a half hour.

"I have to run off to talk to Miriam then back home." Tallah kissed Sashenka's temple as though she was her mother and not her sister. I felt how close they were and then a pang of need to see Meira. "I wish I could stay longer, but please make sure you Skype me, Syd." She waved as she headed for the door. "Have a great first semester, you two."

I grinned at Sashenka as Tallah disappeared. "You've been here longer than me, looks like. Unpacked already?"

The smile on Sashenka's face was gone in a heartbeat. "I... yes." Her energy shifted all of a sudden, from cheerful if nervous to downright awkward. What the hell?

I paused, waiting for more. Sashenka just shifted from foot to foot, no longer meeting my gaze. Um, hello? What happened?

"Guess I have my own unpacking to do." I turned slowly from her, expecting her to say something. Anything. But Sashenka just bobbed her head, spun and rushed from the room.

"Lovely." I sighed and rolled my eyes at Charlotte. "Any clue what I did?"

The weregirl's gaze went to the door, face thoughtful. "No," she said.

Sometimes she frustrated me so much I wanted to shake her.

"Fine," I snapped, good mood shattered, hopes for a happy year fading yet again. "If you don't mind, I have unpacking to do."

Charlotte's expression flattened out and she nodded. She covered the distance from me to the door in three strides. I heard another door open and close firmly, presumably across the hall.

Whatever. She could be as pissy as she wanted. I didn't ask her to come here.

Having fun yet? Gram's magic wrapped me up, amusement obvious.

I snarled to myself as I kicked one of the heavy suitcases. *Yeah. Sure. Peachy keen.*

Demon child, she sent. *Have some faith. In yourself. In this new adventure.*

I sank to the corner of my new bed, struggling with tears. *I don't really need to be here,* I sent back. *I could just come home.*

Gram snorted. *Like you've ever quit on anything in your whole life. Don't start now.*

She was right. And it's not like I hadn't faced worse. It was just... *I was hoping things would be different.* Better. But so far, same old.

Whiner. Gram's tone was mild, but the accusation cut.

Yeah. Guilty.

She left me with a hug and a promise to keep me posted if anything happened in Wilding Springs. Like anything catastrophic requiring my particular skill set to deal with it. I could handle catastrophic, oddly. Had been through enough messes, disasters, near world-ending experiences that being in danger was the norm for me. This having to fit in stuff? I always sucked at it, no matter where we moved to, how many places, how many new schools.

And yet, this was different. I'd be with other witches, so the natural repellant nature of my power wouldn't be in play, the awkward feeling normals had around me no longer an issue. The students I'd be in classes with would be just like me.

Yeah, time to pull it together. So my roommate might not like me and was just pretending so her coven leader sister wouldn't know. Big deal. I could handle it.

I shoved one of the boxes to make more room for myself and had to catch it before it fell. Still, a few things tumbled out, retrieved by my magic. Two photos, one framed in silver, the other in black, hovered before me and I found myself smiling again at last.

The first was of Liam and me, standing under the archway at Wilding Springs High. Prom. He looked hot in his tux and vest, silver satin tie matching my shimmering dress. As much as my memory of prom from the year before had sucked, being dumped by Brad when my lack of power no longer attracted the football hottie, this year's graduation, mine and Liam's, was so much fun I actually hadn't wanted the night to end.

The other, chunky black frame rough around the edges, made my stomach tighten in a good way, my heart melt. Quaid sat on his motorcycle, dressed in delicious leather, the smirk I used to hate and now loved on his handsome face. I took it out of the air, ran my fingertips over his face, felt the connection between us thrum as I focused on him. The picture of Liam settled in my left hand then and, as I looked back and forth between them, I missed them both terribly, but in different ways. I knew Liam would love it here at Harvard and wished he could have joined me. As for Quaid, I just wanted to feel his arms around me, the way our power melded together, the caramel yumminess of him when he kissed me.

My need for Quaid was strongest. On impulse, hoping he was here on campus already and no longer at the summer training camp, I reached down the connection to him.

And found him laughing. But about what? Before I had a chance to explore further, his humor shut off abruptly, his public mind now closed though his magic reached out, full focus now on me.

A tiny hint of worry at what he hid from me was crushed under the rush of love he sent my way.

I miss you. I wish it didn't come out so soft and fragile. Whiny. I hated whiny.

I miss you too. He didn't seem to have the same problem expressing himself. *Are you at school?*

I looked around the room, sighed. *Just arrived. Are you here yet?*

Not yet. A foreign touch of magic, just a thread, stirred along our connection, but Quaid abruptly cut it off. *I'm on my way. Should be there in the morning.*

Who are you with? Yeah, way to sound needy and jealous, Syd. But Quaid just sent more love.

I'll introduce you to the bunch when we arrive, he sent. *You'll like them, Syd. I already told them all about you.*

That made me feel better. *I can't wait to see you.* Not whiny this time. Just true.

Me too. I love you.

Heart singing, I hugged him with my power. *I love you too. So much.*

See you the second I get there. Again that touch of foreign power. *I have to go.*

Yeah, me too. I'm sure he knew I was lying. *See you soon.*

His magic released me gently as he left. Why then did it hurt so much when he was gone?

Unpacking took less time than I expected and it wasn't long before everything I had was in order. Turned out all the clothes fit perfectly inside the wardrobe, no doubt a quirk of living on a witch floor. Just when I thought I couldn't stuff one more sweater inside, the hangers parted and room was made. As I stood back to close the door, I realized how much of a clotheshorse I'd actually become.

Alison's fault. I shied from thinking about her, setting the photos of the boys next to the one of Meira and me last Halloween, Gram sticking her tongue out at the camera in the background. I frowned a little, remembering how I'd looked for a picture of Mom, something to bring with me, but hadn't been able to find one. Of Dad, either. Though my vampire Uncle Frank and his undead girlfriend Sunny graced my night stand.

I pondered my computer. It would be easy to spend the rest of the afternoon and evening lost in video games or TV shows, but I felt the need to escape the room, to get out and explore. The moment I set tentative foot outside my door, Charlotte's whipped open and she strode out to meet me.

She didn't say anything, just waited, blonde hair rippling with her slow, steady breathing. There were times, like this one, when she reminded me far more of the wolf she could become than the girl she was.

"Hungry?" I didn't wait for her to answer, knowing she wouldn't bother. Charlotte was a person of few words and even fewer emotions, at least those that showed on her face or body. I'd gotten used to her stillness and quiet, the stoic way she did everything as though she was a carefully carved statue, much like the one housing my father's soul when he crossed from Demonicon. But with Charlotte it was training, not stone or metal, causing her to appear so precise and near perfect.

She trailed behind me as I stepped out into the Yard. I'd given up asking her to walk beside me long ago. Despite my insistence we be friends, Charlotte never treated me as anything but someone she had to protect at all costs.

Hard to be chummy with her when I knew she would kill anyone who crossed my path the wrong way, guilty of a crime or not.

Harvard Square called me, full of shops and cafes. We

sat together at least and enjoyed a delicious bowl of pasta, though Charlotte naturally didn't show if she liked it one way or the other, gaze constantly roving the surrounds though her body seemed perfectly relaxed. I knew the opposite. Had first-hand experience with her particular brand of body guarding. Trying to clear the memory of a pair of football jocks back home who thought it would be funny to sneak up behind me and scare me.

Yeah, I wasn't scared. For myself. It took a few minutes to stop her, but by then they were already screaming.

Fun times in Wilding Springs.

As I dug into my meal, I suppressed a pang of guilt. I could have just gone to see Mom and Meira, had dinner with them. Or, at least, I assumed that was the case. But I needed a bit of time on my own, now that I'd shaken off my needy new girlness. And even when I'd finished my exploration of the square, returned to the Yard and passed Massachusetts Hall where Mom and my sister, demon cat Sassafras with them, were living, I kept going. The sun was just going down and I felt drained from the trip and my own upended emotions. Mom and I had our disastrous moments at the best of times, especially now she'd taken on the Council Leadership. The last thing I wanted was to top off my first day with a nuclear argument.

The bathroom I shared with Sashenka was a generous size, the shower larger than I'd expected, a tiled stall with a seat built in. The double sinks left me enough room for my paltry collection of toiletries. I felt slightly in awe of the bags and cases of things on Sashenka's side, all neatly arranged, but not as much as I might have a few years ago. I'd grown accustomed to such things because of Alison.

Again with the ghostly best friend avoidance. I really had to do something about her, if only when I thought of my dead friend I didn't have to feel guilt at keeping the echo of who she was here because of my own selfishness.

Teeth brushed, I spent an hour or so on my computer before sliding under the covers and turning off the light over my bed. Sashenka still wasn't back and I found myself stewing. I finally had to turn over on my side, back to the door, and force myself into deep breathing so my temper would cool enough I wouldn't attack her the moment she appeared.

Things were supposed to be different. Despite the warnings from all the well-meaning witches I'd spoken to, I was really hoping for a new best friend. I missed Alison most in the times when I just wanted another girl to talk to and, as naive as my expectations may have been, I was hoping my roommate might fill that void. Especially once

I knew it was Sashenka. But now all the expectations were disappointments.

I was tired enough the tactic finally worked, lulling me into sleep.

A shrill scream jerked me out of a happy dream about a green meadow and something to do with butterflies that looked like Liam. My demon roared to wakefulness, shoving me up and out of bed, to land on the floor in a protective crouch while Shaylee's Sidhe power called to the earth to ground us. The family magic quivered around me, threads of amber and green tracing through the blue as my eyes scanned the dark room, just enough light from my summoned power to show me the source of the scream.

Sashenka sat on the floor next to her bed, dark eyes huge, staring, mouth still open though her shriek cut off abruptly, her bed clothes piled on top of her. The door swung open, Charlotte bounding into the room, only to freeze as she took in the scene.

"Nightmare." Charlotte relaxed. "Are you well, Miss Hensley?"

Sashenka shuddered, but looked embarrassed as she pulled herself up from the floor. "I'm so sorry," she said. "It must have been." Her neat and tidy sheets and quilt were a shambles, tangled up, half jerked to the floor themselves as if she'd fought someone in her dream. "Forgive me for waking you." Her dark eyes turned to me, but wouldn't meet mine.

I huffed in irritation, but not because I was awake. "As long as you're okay." I waved to Charlotte who left without a word, pulling the door solidly shut behind her.

"Yes, yes, I'm fine, of course." Sashenka climbed back into bed. "I'm so sorry."

For what? Seriously, what was her problem? And was she crying?

"It's okay," I said, trying to rein in my frustration. What was wrong with her? "Do you want to talk about it?"

She shook her head so fiercely I just shrugged to myself.

I slid into bed, curled up with my back to her, the same position I'd just left. I had to find a way to get her to talk to me, even if it was only to tell me she didn't like me. That had to be it. She put on a show for Tallah, but now it was just the two of us, Sashenka obviously didn't know how to say it. And here she was, trapped with a coven leader she couldn't stand. Must be nice for her.

But before I could go to poor me, my anger wicked. She had no reason not to like me! I was awesome. Maybe it was some kind of hold-over from what Mom did, saving Dad by hiding the fact he'd used blood magic. But Tallah didn't hold that against me. In fact, the entire Council ruled in favor of pardoning Mom as long as she took over leadership.

I was about to roll over and confront the other girl, still sniffling in her bed, when she shrieked again.

This time I was on my feet and at her side before she stopped screaming. I crouched next to her, taking her hands and pulling her up. "What happened?"

Sashenka shook so much her long, dark hair swung around her hips. "I don't know." She burst into tears and fled from me, running to the bathroom. The light switched on, illumination cut off when she slammed the door behind her, only a crack of it showing through the bottom.

Great. Hysterical for no reason. Maybe it wasn't me. Maybe she was just nuts.

At least I had experience with mentally unbalanced. Speaking of which, I was about to reach for Gram for advice, her being the Queen of Crazy at one point, when something cold brushed against my chest.

And the gem holding the vampire virus.

Normally I would have felt guilty about what I was about to do, but I was still angry, the confrontation I'd planned with Sashenka cut short, so instead of being gentle I opened my magic and snatched the echo from the air, jerking Alison into view.

So she'd followed me after all. And was obviously the source of Sashenka's lack of sleep and floor tumbles. Alison must have been learning to use the bits of power she'd stolen from the virus before I'd shielded it against her.

"Al," I said, letting her hear how mad I was even as the bathroom door opened and my roommate entered. I heard Sashenka gasp while Alison's lips twisted into a smirk.

She'd changed, the ghostly remains of her distilling into her most negative traits. Petulance lined her face, pulling down her forehead, darkening her smirk even as she struggled to be the girl she'd been before she died. I could tell she fought against accepting she was dead, had been over this with her in the past. But she *was* dead, most likely a suicide, and the last remains of her refused to let go.

I turned to Sashenka. "I'm the one who's sorry," I said. "Alison isn't supposed to be here."

Sashenka hugged herself, pity in her eyes. "It's all right," she whispered.

"No, it's not." I was in no mood to be kind, gaze returning to what remained of my best friend, summoned by Gram performing the necromancy she needed to save Mom's life during the trial. Alison hadn't been called, not like Quaid's parents or my grandfather or even Naudia Purity. She'd simply been newly dead and felt me near her and came across herself. I should have sent her back then, but how could I when I still blamed myself for not being there for my best friend when she needed me? But at the moment all of my guilt and good will was nowhere to be felt.

Alison squirmed in the grip of my power, transparency more obvious as she used strength against me in an attempt to escape. "I was just kidding around." She focused on Sashenka, tried for a patented Alison Morgan 100-watt smile, but it fell far short, as much a ghost of reality as she was. "You know me, Syd. I'm just a kidder."

Desperation in her voice, the need to be accepted. And yet, the darkness in her would never let her rest. I knew it, it tormented me. But this wasn't the time or the place to deal with it.

"Just leave Sashenka alone." I stepped back from Alison while her eyes narrowed and her generous mouth puckered.

"New bestie, Syd?" Alison's hiss had power behind it as she swayed just above the floor. "Traitor."

I sighed, all my anger draining away even as I let her go. "Just stop, Al. Please. You know you need to move on. Don't make me force you."

She snarled at me, rushed me, but even as I raised my hands in an automatic gesture to ward her off, she shifted directions and blew through Sashenka before vanishing.

Another round of apologies to my roommate did nothing to thaw the tension between us. Out of energy and really not caring anymore, I left Sashenka shivering and saying *she* was sorry—for what I had no idea—to once again curl up with my back to her.

This time when I tried to call up sleep it ignored me completely. Partly because my demon was still riled and even Shaylee upset by what happened with Alison. I did my best to reassure them, but neither was really talking to me, so I just let them stew and settled into my own version.

My thoughts went instead to Alison, to the vampire virus trapped in the jewel I wore around my neck. I glanced down at it, the softest of glows escaping the piles of shields I'd placed around it. I felt it at times, stirring, though there was no way it could break free. Or so I told myself.

Despite what Dad said when he gave me the thing, trapped in a marble of stone after he and Theridialis tried to contain it on Demonicon, it turned out Sebastian and the vampires were unable to destroy it. In fact, Sebastian had a hard time being around me now, a fact which made me very sad. I adored the beautiful blood clan leader, was happy I'd found a way to free him from the prison he'd made of his body in an attempt to contain the very same virus. But the call of it, what remained of its residual energy inside him, pulled him in a way that made us both uncomfortable.

Even Sunny and Uncle Frank had no luck. When they tried to touch it, the thing attacked them, shields or no shields, able to use its power on them despite my attempts to keep it under control. As long as it wasn't around vampires, it seemed content to remain contained so we decided—I decided—it was best if I dealt with it.

Yay me. Taking responsibility. Which meant I was stuck with the thing until I could figure out a way to kill it once and for all.

I knew it was the virus attracting Alison. She'd discovered, shortly after her echo appeared, the power inside it could keep her aware and partially corporeal unlike most ghosts. And now she craved it, came for it fairly frequently. I poured more shields over it as I lay there, smothering it further, until the faint glow was only visible if I didn't look directly at it, a mirage in my peripheral vision.

Who knew what would happen if Alison was able to access its full power? I shuddered under the warmth of my blankets, suddenly chilled to the bone. It was bad enough the virus itself wanted to consume others. What would it be able to do as a vampire ghost? Was such a thing even possible?

Would Alison live again as pure undead? The thought made me pause, and this wasn't the first time. What if I did let her have it? Would my friend really be alive?

I already knew the answer. The girl I knew, the real essence of who she was, was long gone, passed over. This echo could never be allowed to take control of the virus.

The marble stirred over my heart and I found myself quickly clenching one hand around it. It shouldn't be stirring, not with the amount of magic I had cushioning it. It wasn't like there were vampires here to attract it, either. No vampires were allowed in Harvard Yard.

After a moment, the virus fell still again and I slid the gem back inside my T-shirt. Finally worn out enough to sleep, I fell into a dreaming state dominated by blood-soaked vampires, sobbing Sashenka and the gaping, laughing face of the girl who had once been my best friend.

I woke to the sound of the door closing and, groggy from

my terrible sleep, flipped over to find Sashenka's bed made and her missing.

Lovely. Just freaking lovely. Well, at least I didn't have to see her much. Today was first day of classes already and, aside from sleeping in the same room, I could keep our interactions to a minimum if that was what she wanted.

Grumpy and out of sorts, wishing I'd come the day before instead of leaving my trip to the last minute, I slid out of bed and hit the shower.

The hot water helped improve my mood a little. By the time I'd dressed, I even felt human. Never mind I'd never admit how carefully I'd chosen my clothes, the blue sweater Quaid loved, my favorite denim skirt hugging my hips and flaring to my knees. I even took the time to run the flat-iron through my hair and double up on my mascara layer and lip gloss. Pathetic, really. Quaid proved over and over he loved me no matter what I looked like. Still, I was feeling the need, after not seeing him for so long, to show off a little.

So sue me.

Computer and a blank notebook tucked in my bag and I was on my way, Charlotte on my heels. The hall was quiet, though a few late witches ran past me, down to mingle with the normals and outside into the Yard. Not one person paused to smile, say hi, even notice me and the old gloom settled around me even as I stepped out into the sunlight.

Syd's on her own again. Well, isn't that special? Just like always. Years and years of being an outcast had clearly stamped some kind of message across my whole being.

College was supposed to be different. And yet, obviously it wasn't the case.

Two steps in the sunshine and I shook myself.

Yes, this year was different. I had Charlotte, for one thing. So I was never alone. I tried to see that as a consoling fact and caught myself grinning. Sure, she wasn't the best conversationalist, but at least I had someone I could bounce ideas off of, eat meals with.

Maybe if people saw me with someone else they'd take a chance. I was determined to make some friends this year, if only to replace the ones I'd lost, the brief and shining friendships I fought at first and now cherished the memories of now that they were gone.

Beth with her cute bob and sweet nature was at state college with her boyfriend Tim, thanks to Mom and a scholarship from the Brindle family in England. Blood was gone to Europe with his family, the tall, looming Goth with his deep voice and steady, calming nature that always made me smile. Pain, Mia, the lost daughter of the Dumont coven, now their leader. She was lost to me in more ways than one and I found I missed her a great deal. Alison. Not going there. And Simon.

I perked. Simon! He was here at Harvard, had been bumped years ahead, only fifteen and now a sophomore. I was sure I'd find him at some point. The idea of seeing his sweet face, thick glasses perched on his narrow nose, skinny body all arms and legs, made everything all right again.

Simon was the type who would have made friends, the outcast kind. And those, it turned out, were the ones I liked the most.

Grinning at the thought of falling into another group of quirky, funny, genuine friends thanks to Simon, I headed across campus with a lighter heart.

Memorial Hall loomed over me, the wide wings flanking the massive tower in the center making me nauseous all of a sudden. What was I thinking coming here? Trying to fit in with other kids, even witches, when I was so... not like them?

I think I would have turned around and hidden in my room if it hadn't been for Charlotte. She must have sensed my panic because she grasped my arm firmly, one of the rare times she'd ever touched me, and guided me forward through the big doors to face my destiny.

Well, breakfast. Annenberg Hall stretched out in front of me, all carved wood and arching ceiling beams and stunning stained glass, so gorgeous and overwhelming I stood there a long moment, just taking in the sight. Most of the tables were full, but at least no one paid attention to me as I gaped like an idiot at the view.

Charlotte got me moving again even as the tingle of magic in the place suddenly made me feel calm. There was power here, not just in the building, but in the students around me.

I'd felt them last night, of course, but I'd been in the middle of my own stuff and didn't really pay attention. I was paying attention now. I felt them, all different degrees of magic, as I made my way down the center aisle and gathered up my own breakfast.

Charlotte and I found a place at the end of a table. Okay, Charlotte made us a place and I took the seat vacated by the nervous freshman who took one look at my bodyguard and gulped the last of his milk before grabbing his tray and running like a rabbit.

As we sat, I caught the faintest glimmer of a smile on the weregirl's face and found myself laughing.

"You enjoy that, don't you?" The scrambled eggs and sausage smelled great, toast slightly soggy. I sniffed my yogurt as I peeled back the top while Charlotte delicately began to eat her bacon, eggs, sausages and ham with her fingers.

"Sometimes." Humor shone in her eyes for a moment. "It's so easy."

I nodded, sipping my orange juice. "I hear you."

Maybe she was warming up to me, would be more willing to be my friend after all. But when I tried to talk to her further, Charlotte just continued to eat, gaze flat, face a mask of nothing.

Which left me time to think. Never a good idea. Especially when I hadn't yet heard from Quaid. Hadn't he promised to contact me the second he arrived? Did that mean he was here, but was avoiding me? Or worse, that he hadn't arrived, because he wasn't coming? Or couldn't because he was hurt or sick or...? Fear grappled with doubt grappled with anxiety until I could barely swallow.

A quick glance at my watch told me I was about to be late for my first class on my first day and didn't have time to worry about my absent boyfriend. The cafeteria emptied out quickly, leaving Charlotte and I in the softy echoing room, the vastness of it making me feel very small.

I briefly considered riding the veil to class, but rules were rules. Besides, even if I could, doing so would only draw attention to myself and the last thing I wanted this year was any kind of attention. Instead I raced back across Cambridge Street with Charlotte right behind me and through the Yard toward Widener Library.

I didn't have time to admire the massive white columns or the wide steps and huge doorways as I raced up the stairs and into the building, the smaller libraries flanking the gigantic place vanishing as I hurried through the doors. A pang of thought for Liam and how much he would have loved to explore the place was fleeting as I stopped, out of breath, and stared into the perfectly normal-looking, if massive and oppressive, foyer leading into the main library.

The coolest part about Harvard was how both witches and normal students and faculty were able to co-exist. Most buildings had a magic component of some kind to them, specifically for my kind, off limits to normals. But for the most part, including the cafeteria and some of the classes, we mingled together like we were all one big, happy campus.

Case in point was Widener Library. The majority of it was for normals, housing a gazillion or so books. But the witches who had a hand in creating it were sure to include one very important detail—Coven Hall. I was allowed to attend normal classes if I chose, or could simply do my three years of witch studies and be done. I still hadn't decided if I wanted to give biology or calculus a try, but I wasn't closed to the idea.

I knew what to do, had it drilled into me when Mom filled me in on what the campus was like, but it still bothered me being unfamiliar where I was about to go.

Just as I drew a breath and turned left, headed for a plain wooden door looking more like the entry to a janitor's closet than a class for witches, a skinny guy with lank, dark hair raced around me and jerked the door open, slamming it shut behind him. Just like that. I glanced around, just in case, though I knew there was no way a normal would care what he just did thanks to the magic protecting it, nor could someone without power repeat it. The magic keeping the area safe deflected the eyes of those without power and prevented them from stumbling on the doorway hiding the space where reality existed and magic began.

Despite knowing it was much like how we used to protect our coven site, I still felt a shiver go down my spine as I strode forward and opened the door, passing through the shields, emerging inside a dark but lofty hallway, the ceiling reaching high above me, wood paneled walls much like those on the rest of the campus.

Coven Hall was to be my school for the next three years.

The hall stretched out before me, feeling endless. Probably was endless, when it came down to it. Door upon ornately carved wooden door flanked the wide corridor, my footsteps muffled in the thick black carpet running on and on forever deeper into Coven Hall. How was I supposed to figure out which class was mine?

Power flickered and a wide-bottomed older woman with hair the same color as her fuchsia dress popped into view. She floated just above the floor, foot-tall body shimmering with energy.

"Class schedule?" Her voice was tinkly soft, but clearly understandable. I'd never seen a sprite before, or even for a moment thought I'd ever meet one. She pondered my list a moment, whipping out a pair of horn-rimmed glasses, also deeply pink, before tapping the paper with one index finger. It flickered, the page turning black before the sprite floated close, a perfect bow smile on her little pink lips.

"Freshmen." She rolled her eyes. No way. Her irises were pink, too. How weird was that? But she giggled like a little girl despite her aged appearance and I found myself grinning. "Here you are, Sydlynn Hayle." I took the page back from her. "Have a wonderful semester."

The moment my fingers touched the page everything shifted sideways. I had to catch my balance to keep from falling as the whole corridor jerked to the left, then the right before the world slammed into place.

A very different reality faced me. Instead of being in an endless hallway, I now stood in the center of a circular room of eight doors. The one behind me was closed, but the others stood open, all bustling with activity inside. Each was marked in large block numbers, one through seven.

Charlotte actually choked on a giggle before schooling her features again and I tried not to feel insulted. Clearly, class one was my first of the day. As I strode through the door with an outward confidence I didn't feel, I did my best to pretend a foot-tall sprite with a propensity for pink hadn't just treated me like an idiot.

I knew from a previous look at my schedule I'd just walked into Elemental Studies with Blanche Rhodes as my instructor. I wasn't sure what to expect, though the Rhodes coven, led by Violet, were allies as long as I didn't break the law. The adorable old lady who led the Rhodes coven was a stickler for playing things by the rules.

My goal was to slip inside and take a seat at the back, avoid notice and slip out again in the mass of students, just like always. But, because I was late, it turned out I was the last student to arrive. That coupled with my aggressive entrance, my bodywere at my back, drew every single eye.

Including Blanche's. The moment she saw me I knew, without a moment of doubt, I was in for a very, very bad year.

Her brown eyes lit up like her long-lost granddaughter had just come home. The portly woman held out both hands to me, a smile on her cherub face, perfectly coiffed hair piled high, not moving a bit as she took three steps toward me.

"Look who we have, class!" Those hands pulled toward her, tucking under her chin as she clasped them together in sheer delight. "I saw your name on my roster, but I couldn't believe for a moment you'd be here." Blanche gestured for me to join her at the front and a single seat left wide open in the middle.

For me.

Oh no.

I could run. There was still time. Until I heard the door swing shut and slam behind me. Blanche was hurrying to my side by then, hands grasping mine, hers moist and warm, the skin almost doughy. I fought the urge to pull myself free, struggling with what to do, how to save myself as she guided me down the steps to the front of the lecture hall and presented me to the class.

"Everyone," she gushed, trembling beside me, "may I present Sydlynn Hayle, the leader of the Hayle coven and your classmate." Blanche clapped her hands, the meaty smack making me wince. No one looked impressed, though I did my best not to meet any eyes.

I was too busy begging the elements to swallow me whole.

When no one reacted, Blanche's face fell a little. "Well then, Sydlynn, dear," she guided me to the "special" seat, making sure I was comfortable before backing up a few steps and smiling at the class. "Shall we begin?"

Blanche Rhodes wasn't a terrible teacher. In fact, she

would have been fine if she was standing in front of five year olds.

"Now then," she said, slowly, with exaggerated carefulness. "We're going to be discussing the elements and what they can do." She looked around the group, eyes bright, smile wide. "Does everyone know what an element is?"

She wasn't freaking serious. I'd avoided using or having anything to do with magic up until I was forced to at sixteen and even then I knew what an element was.

Painful silence. Well, at least I wasn't the focus of attention anymore. Let the freshmen witches just forget all about me in the front row and instead put their attention on the embarrassment happening before them.

It wasn't until Blanche's gaze settled on me I understood the full brunt of what was to be my endless torture in her class.

"Sydlynn," she said. "Since you're a coven leader," she drew the two words out like it was something amazing, winking broadly at the class, "why don't you tell us what the elements are."

The next hour and a half dragged out in a spiraling downward collapse, and by the time it was over, the door swinging open to let us out, I was so overcome by the fact I would never, ever make friends with any other witches

I just sat there and let the others leave so I didn't have to even be near them.

I felt the animosity toward me, how every single student in the class blamed me for the brain-numbing lecture a baby would understand, with me as the mouthpiece of a woman who shouldn't be allowed to train dogs to bark.

Blanche rushed forward to take my hands and help me to my feet.

"I can't wait for tomorrow." She clapped her hands again after setting me free. "You were wonderful, my dear. Now, off with you." She gestured to the door where a few students were trickling in. "I have another class to teach."

Torture. Surely she meant torture. The exit wasn't nearly close enough for my liking.

I paused in the round room, eyes fixed on door number two. There was another door next to it, marked "café", but no way was I was risking it. Better to creep into my next class and hide.

Just as I set foot on the threshold, I caught movement out of the corner of my eye and turned my head. Jean Marc and Kristophe Dumont waved at me from the entry to the diner.

"Well done, *mon cher*," Jean Marc said.

"*Oui*," Kristophe struck one of his model poses, long

hair swinging over his shoulder as he fixed me with his disgusting gaze. "You were the teacher's pet, *non*?"

Choke. What? How did I miss they were in my class? They both exited the cafe, heading for me.

For door number two.

As they brushed past me, Kristophe licked his lips, Jean Marc's smirk turning my stomach.

"Let's see if you can be a little less obvious, shall we?" Kristophe's fingers brushed over my hair as the two entered the class, laughing, Kristophe glancing back over his shoulder.

I didn't know I was shaking until Charlotte's steady hand found my elbow. She pulled me forcefully aside, lips near my ear.

"If he touches you again, I kill him."

I met her eyes, saw the hate deep inside her. Emotion at last. And I hardly blamed her. The Dumonts enslaved Charlotte's people, divided them when her father, Raoul, and part of the pack were freed by Galleytrot.

"No," I said, voice more steady than it should have been. "If Kristophe touches me again, I'll kill him. You can have Jean Marc."

She actually seemed to be considering it a moment. When she finally nodded, I actually smiled. Way to ease the tension.

A rush of students pushed past me as I turned, my bodywere at my back, to enter the class. Naturally I was now one of the last inside. I had a lot to thank the brothers for and this was just one more slice of joy.

At least the teacher of my Mixed Magics lab wasn't crazy. But, she was an ally, too, at least from an ally family. Easton Hensley smiled at me as I entered, but didn't go all freakazoid, thank goodness. She let me find my own seat, at a low table with two stools, the one beside me vacant. I looked around, caught students staring and realized, with a huge surge of regret, most of them had been in my last class.

This was going to suck.

"Students, you'll be pairing up." Easton's magic sent slips of black paper flying toward each of us. I glanced down at my page, saw a list of names. As the people around me started pairing off, their names disappeared like magic—okay, it was magic—from the page until only my name remained.

Oh. My. Swearword.

What was this, elementary school? No one wanted to pick me for their team? Fine.

I didn't care what anyone said, witches were as big a jerks as normals.

Easton's discomfort was obvious. "We normally have

an even number of students," she said as if that made a difference. "Last minute drop out."

I bet. The Brothers Jerk sniggered at me from two tables behind and I wanted to spin and smash them both into the ground. So did my demon. And Shaylee. And Charlotte from the way she watched them like they might be tasty to eat once she'd gutted them.

Easton was nice enough as we proceeded with the lab, most of what we were doing pretty basic so I could handle it on my own. But the isolation was getting to me, the way the others glanced my way when they thought I wasn't looking. The whispers and giggling and the growing sense I wasn't wanted, actively disliked in fact, forcing me to raise a shell of protection around myself.

That old familiar shell I'd worn in high school.

Damn it.

At least the defensive and offensive magics Easton had us practicing were an outlet for my hurt. And though I'm sure my proficiency and the power behind each technique, from raising glowing shields humming with multiple layers of power to blowing apart a candle inside a warded space, wasn't endearing me to my classmates, by the time the door swung open to let us out, I didn't give a crap what any of them thought.

I left the moment I could, ahead of them all, not bothering to thank Easton for the class. I felt a little badly about that, considering how nice and not all gooey she'd been to me. Instead, I marched right to the exit door and out into the real world again, head held high though my soul quivered unhappily inside me.

Lunch was another quiet hunch in the impressive cafeteria followed by a slow, slumping return across the Yard toward the library and more torture. I was recognizing faces at least. Yeah, sure was. Only because those faces glared at me like I was some kind of freak who'd ruined everything.

The really crappy part in all of this was how so very far I'd really come. I wasn't the complaining, poor-me girl who wanted to be normal anymore. I really felt like I'd grown up a lot in the last two years, learned things about myself, who I was and, more importantly, who I could be some day. And I'd embraced my future, or at least told myself I had.

Why then was it back to the same old, same old with me retreating all over again, afraid, willing to not be me just for a chance to fit in? Nothing about how I was feeling felt right or natural anymore. Sucked how easy it was to backslide into old habits.

I felt my shoulders go back, lifted my chin again on

purpose, but this time not to hide the struggle inside, but to face the world and be okay with who I was. Let them judge me, criticize behind their backs, make assumptions. This Hayle witch had saved her family, the world twice and had a Sidhe Gatekeeper and a vampire blood clan leader as friends. Not to mention a hound of the Wild Hunt and a mother who led the entire North American Council and a father now in line for the rulership of Demonicon.

I had nothing to be ashamed of or nervous about.

Charlotte chuffed softly behind me. I could feel her approval sliding outward to touch me and wondered just how close her bond to me really was. I'd never considered maybe there could be more to her guarding me than just the physical. Had she attached herself to me in some way magically? If so, it was a one-way street. And that made me sad.

I stopped and turned to face her, so fast she actually looked surprised for a flash of an instant. Score.

"Listen," I said, my confidence back with a vengeance. "I'm tired of this slave/master crap you've got going on."

Charlotte looked like I'd slapped her and I wondered what boundary I'd just stepped over.

"I'm not your slave," she whispered.

Hmmm. Not exactly what I meant, but I understood

at least. The Dumonts held her and her family in literal slavery. Clearly our relationship was nothing like that.

I actually tsked in frustration that she'd chosen to go there. "You know exactly what I mean."

She glanced away from what I hoped was my steely gaze after a moment and sighed. "I do," she said.

"Okay then." Arms crossed over my chest, I prodded her with magic. My demon hummed softly, reaching for her and, to my surprise, Charlotte opened up and let me in. A little. But enough for me to see just how much control she had over herself on the surface, hiding a churning wealth of emotion underneath.

She firmly pushed my demon back and closed off the connection. "I'm responsible for you," she said. "My family owes you a debt. As our pack leader, my father should be fulfilling this role."

We'd had this conversation, back when she'd saved my life when my little blue Cooper Mini exploded during Mom's trial, thanks to Jean Marc and Kristophe playing with explosives. Charlotte told me she owed me then.

But she was forgetting part of that particular conversation. "I told you we were going to be friends," I said. "That I don't want or need a bodywere."

A tiny smile quirked the corner of her mouth at the term

I don't think I'd ever spoken aloud, but she nodded slowly. "I remember," she said. "But Sydlynn, I'm your protector. And whether you know it or not, accept it or not, you are an important person, with a great destiny. It's the job of those like me to make sure you are able to do what you need to without worry for your safety."

That was the longest speech I'd ever heard from her. Not to mention she'd just told me what she thought of me. Great destiny? Yeah, if I could somehow stop stumbling from one disaster to another, maybe.

I took a step closer to her, in her space but not crowding her, just enough she could feel the pulse of my power around me and how little I thought of her need to protect me.

"I need friends more than bodyguards," I said. "And if you're going to be around me all the time, I'd really like for you to be someone I can talk to."

Charlotte's cheeks pinked, her gaze sliding from mine before she met my eyes again. She was smiling, a real smile, not a half-hidden grin or a sarcastic, momentary smirk. The pleasure lit her eyes and made me smile too.

"I'll try," she said, voice soft and girly, not the usual flat, controlled tone she typically used, making me wonder just how young she was. "When you said that, last time, I thought… I didn't think you meant it."

Her accent was more pronounced, the eastern-European influence of her birthplace showing up as she let down her guard. I took it as a great sign.

"Well," I said, turning and hooking my arm through hers, forcing her to walk beside me as we moved on. "I did. And I do. Friends."

Her gait wasn't as smooth as I was used to and I know what I was doing made her uncomfortable, but she was softer, in her expressions, in her whole being, so I was fairly sure I'd gotten through to her at last.

Even when I released her arm she stayed at my side, no longer following three steps behind.

I loved winning arguments. Especially since I didn't very often.

The day was looking up. And when I heard a familiar voice call my name, I actually did a double take, wondering why the tall, handsome guy with the almost shaved head triggered a moment of recognition. He lumbered to a halt, breathing a little heavy, dark eyes smiling as much as his wide mouth, tanned skin glowing with good health. He shifted his backpack over one wide shoulder before reaching out to hug me.

Um. Hello? Hug me? I retreated immediately, Charlotte falling right back into protection mode though this time I didn't mind. Not that I needed her help, but the guy kind of freaked me out.

His eyes flew wide, hurt crossing his face a moment before he froze. And started to laugh.

I knew that laugh. Knew it. But from where? Nothing about this guy seemed familiar at all. I'm sure I would have recognized him if we'd met before, especially if he knew me well enough he thought hugging would be acceptable. There weren't many people who fell into my "willing to touch" category.

"Syd," he said, voice dropping to a low, slow drawl, chin tucking down as he purposely stooped his big shoulders and let his head bob up and down a little.

Cogs ground, gears made connections, that voice, my name spoken, the way he carried himself. It couldn't possibly be. But it was.

"Blood?" His name came out in a squeal of girlie joy as I lunged forward and hugged him. My Goth friend—well, former Goth—was definitely on my huggable list.

He picked me up, swung me around, set me back down, still laughing. "Hey, Syd."

I forced myself to take a step back, not bothering to hide my shock as I looked him up and down. "The last time I saw you—"

"I was the King of Emo." Blood grinned. "Yeah, sorry about that." His natural voice was actually a little higher than I remembered, less gravelly. I grinned, wanting to torture him for being a poser, but let it go in favor of enjoying a happy moment just being with my friend.

It felt like so long ago he and Simon, Pain and Beth had roped me into their peculiar little group, composed of brainiacs, Goths complete with black makeup and pierced everything and fallen cheerleader angels. They were my first real friends and, standing there, looking up at the guy I knew as Blood, all of the nasty, pathetic, horrible stuff that happened today finally faded completely.

"I can't believe it," I said, I'm sure grinning like a lunatic. "Why didn't you tell me you were here?" We still emailed occasionally, though not so much over the summer, not after I told him Alison had died.

"Wanted to surprise you." His grin was just as loopy, so I was in good company. "Worked, right?"

"So worked." I punched his shoulder. Turned suddenly to Charlotte who observed with her flat, empty gaze firmly back in place. She better not have backslid on me or she was in big troubled. "Charlotte, this is…" I turned back to him, suddenly stumped. "You're not Blood anymore," I said. "And you know, I never heard your real first name."

He made a face, one of those long-suffering faces meaning he didn't really want to tell me. "Yeah," he said, one big hand running over the stubble of his hair, a blush rising to his cheeks, "about that." He hesitated one more minute, to which I laughed.

"Dude," I said with as much sarcasm as I could muster, "my mom named me Sydlynn Thaddea. How freaking bad could it be?"

His blush faded, grin back as he nodded. "Rupert." He held his hand out to Charlotte who took it firmly. "Rupert Salinger." He glanced at me, as if expecting me to laugh. He really had to be kidding. I'd heard way worse. "But call me Rupe, yeah?"

"Rupe," I said. "But don't be pissed if I mess up and call you Blood from time to time." I shook my head at myself as he gave me a gentle, lop-sided smile. "Never mind. You look nothing like your old self."

Rupe's head bobbed again, though his shoulders straightened, pulling up to his full height, so tall I had to strain my neck to look up at him. "It's all good, Syd."

"You found each other!" And then Simon was there, just like that, and there was more hugging and smiling. Though I noticed immediately there were also changes in my young, brilliant friend. He'd grown finally, at least two inches over the summer since I saw him at the funeral, and he'd actually put on a little weight, in a good way. Gone was the super skinny kid, all knobby knees and pointy elbows and black glasses.

Speaking of which, as Simon met my gaze, our faces at the same level, I actually noticed his eyes. He blinked furiously a few times, brown eyes watering.

"No glasses." I gently punched his shoulder and he grinned.

"Wicked, right?" His blinking continued at a rapid pace. "New contacts." It made me wonder how comfortable they were. His shoulders went back, chest puffing outward, a slightly arrogant twist to his smile. "They were Darin's idea."

Who? Didn't matter. Suddenly I had part of my posse back together. How cool was that?

"What are you doing in the Yard?" Rupe shifted his backpack again, the thing bulging with books. I hadn't asked him what courses he was taking. Simon either, for that matter.

Simon flushed a little, but his new, strutting posture didn't soften. "Yeah, I know I'm supposed to be in one of the Houses," he said, "but they decided because of my age I should stay in the freshman dorms one more year." He didn't seem deflated by the news, and it made me wonder.

"I'm in Matthew Hall," Rupe said.

Simon's cockiness broke as he grinned again. "Me too! So awesome. You'll love it there." The new arrogance was gone, my old Simon back again as he snorted softly when he laughed. "I can't wait to show you guys around. Harvard is the bomb."

I was about to comment when I heard Charlotte growl next to me, the same instant I felt a touch of magic. Someone prodded my shields even as three guys in designer everything came to a strutting halt beside us.

Simon's whole attitude changed like a switch had been flipped. The arrogance I'd noticed was back, and double what I'd already witnessed, everything about him suddenly bored and snobby.

Simon? Really? I almost snorted a laugh the idea was so preposterous. But the witch who'd invaded my little reunion wasn't anyone to laugh at. Not from the way he pressed his disgusting power against me. It was the equivalent of a solid fondling and worse he thought it was okay to do so. From the way he smirked at me, one cold green eye winking, he was sure I liked it.

Hell, no.

My demon took care of it and I let her, knowing I could get in trouble for it, but confident enough in the fact I was protecting myself I didn't let a little thing like worry stop her from having her way with him. With a deep, vibrating growl, she slashed through the edges of his shields, leaving them gaping wide and bleeding energy out into the world.

Maybe overkill, but he got the message. Fury and terror warred with shock on his face as he struggled to reseal his wards. Every time he did, my demon cut another path through them until his shields hung in tatters around him.

Personal shields aren't something one just creates out of the blue. They are forged over years, built up and fed from personal power. From the condition his were now in, he'd have to start from scratch. Sucked to be him. And since I hadn't actually harmed him any, aside from showing him just how much he needed to learn to respect others, I was fairly confident no one would back him if he decided to complain.

Whoever this witch was, he'd just learned not to piss me off.

All of this happened in the space of a few heartbeats, so my normal friends sensed nothing but the tension between us. As a parting shot to his ego, I took the guy's name from his mind without permission.

Don't ever, ever touch me, jerkoff.

"Darin Mavore." I let his name roll off my lips with

a small smile even as he glared at me like I'd kicked his puppy. Or something more precious. He probably would have preferred I had to the full emasculation I'd just done.

I kind of liked the new and improved me. No more holding back. Evil joy lit my heart as I thought about all the wonderful things I could accomplish now that I didn't give a crap what others thought.

Where were the Dumont brothers again?

Simon broke my train of thought. "Of course you know Darin," he said like it was obvious. "Everyone does. His parents own most of the world or something."

Darin's reptile eyes flickered to Simon and back to me, a calculation in them making me want to allow my demon to finish what she started. He was attractive with his trendy haircut and model's body, but his soul was black under those ruined shields and the very taste of his magic stirred feelings of violence in me. "And you must be Sydlynn Hayle." He nodded his head ever so slightly, meant it as a slight, I was sure of it, but I nodded back, using Mom's most queenly poise.

"Delighted, I'm sure." This was all kinds of fun. Especially since the two witches with Darin wouldn't meet my eyes and seemed afraid. Well, that wasn't so fun. Unless they were creeps like Darin. Then they could bite me.

I turned to Simon, suddenly concerned. What was my normal friend doing hanging out with witches? Especially witches like these? Simon had already circled around Rupe and came to stand next to Darin, like he needed to show where his real loyalties lay.

Heartbreaking. What had Darin done to win so much loyalty from a lost and lonely boy too young to be at college? I was not only determined to find out, when I did, if it involved anything remotely resembling bullying, I would personally see to it that Darin Mavore suffered a slow and painful death.

Darin didn't give me a chance to ask questions. "Heading to the café," he said like he was going to play polo with the queen or something. And I'd thought Rupe was a poser when he wore his Blood persona. Not.

Simon's expression flickered a moment, worry passing over his face.

"Don't you have class?" I wasn't talking to Darin, staring straight at Simon who refused to meet my eyes.

But Darin wasn't about to let me circumvent his authority. "Who are you, his mommy?" The other two witches laughed, but their humor sounded strained. The flush in Simon's cheeks and the anger flickering over his face told me I'd lost with that one statement.

Rupe glanced at me, a little frown pulling the corners of his mouth. "Maybe I'll come with you." He nodded, ever so slightly. Which meant he didn't like Darin's sway over our young friend any more than I did.

Feeling relieved Simon wouldn't be alone, I backed off, but allowed my demon one last chuff at the edge of Darin's shredded shields as she drew a breath as if tasting him and chuckled.

The boys strode off without me, Rupe glancing over his shoulder with a little wave and a roll of his eyes. But Simon never looked back.

Three doors were left open to me when I passed through the entry to my own private hell. Turned out door number four was actually a direct line to the cafeteria and I told myself maybe I should have just taken it in the first place. But that would have meant missing Rupe and Simon and finding out about Darin.

Not to mention the happy hum of satisfaction from my demon. Okay then, long walks to the caf every day it was. Who knew what fun we could have?

I stood there a moment, looking at the doors, closely tempted to wander into number four, just to see what would happen, but decided not to push my luck. I might have been feeling much more myself and even a tad more aggressive than usual—okay a whole bunch more—but I had to go to school here for three years. And since the institution itself hadn't done anything to annoy me I could at least try to play by the rules.

As I strode into my next class behind door number three,

it was with a whole new attitude and from the expressions of those who watched me enter, it was obvious. Did they think me suddenly arrogant? Let them. I honestly couldn't care less.

I moved to a seat near the middle, pulling Charlotte along beside me, pausing to wave at the brothers Dumont who sat in the back, even smiled at them though my demon crawled and muttered and begged to let her loose. I continued smiling, saw the smirks fade from their faces, the slow, fearful frowns growing as I just stood there and stared and smiled.

By the time the two had slunk down in their seats, scowls pulling their handsome faces into petulant masks, I was feeling much, much better. I took my seat without further ado, jerking Charlotte down into the one beside me.

"I'm supposed to stand at the door." She shifted in her chair, clearly uncomfortable. With a sigh, I let her go, not bothering to watch as she slid out of the aisle, knowing she would spend the rest of the class at attention.

I looked up in the sudden quiet and into the nearly black eyes of my next teacher. I'd done some homework, knew the short, round man with the thick head of black hair and skin deepened by race and sun exposure was Isodore Santos. This was my first real experience with anyone from the Santos coven since the trial and I didn't know what to expect. After all, the Santos clan and their leader, Benita, were aligned with the Dumont coven, or had been when Odette was leader. Now that the evil old woman was dead and no longer influencing the Santos family, had things shifted for the better?

Isodore seemed neither hostile nor particularly friendly so I had to assume they had. Either that or he didn't care one way or the other. I'd take it.

Practical magic focused on the use of herbs and natural magic, the way power surrounded us and permeated everything. How the most common of items sometimes contained the most amazing magic. I actually found myself fascinated by the class, conducted in the warm, rich voice of Isodore. A momentary pang of sadness passed over me as I realized why I enjoyed the lecture so much. He reminded me of Martin and Louisa Vega, both practical magic practitioners who had treated me like their own daughter my whole life. Up until they were killed, murdered by Celeste Oberman, a fellow Purity absorbed into our coven. I hadn't thought much of the departed Vegas, lost to a magically fed fire, or Celeste and her traitorous ways, in quite some time. I owed the horse-faced witch some pain and retribution.

The Santos teacher reminded me a bit of Martin and the familiar topic, one both of them were happy to share with me though I was rarely interested, actually helped me calm down and settle despite the memory of the fire and my need to destroy Celeste.

Isodore finally set down the bundle of lavender he'd been holding, the faint green glow from the flower fading. "That's all for now, students. I'll see you tomorrow."

I shook my head, feeling a little muzzy, as though I'd been lost in something. But no, nothing nefarious. He was just a great teacher. The best I'd ever had. Even the rest of the students seemed to agree, not one of them focusing on me, or even looking my way, chatting, normal, happy.

This was college life. This embrace of mixed emotions and magics, a wall of fellow young witches moving from class to class in easy, uncomplicated steps.

I smiled at Charlotte on the way by, pulled her forward to walk beside me, which she did with little effort.

"Sydlynn."

My head snapped around at the whisper of my name. But I didn't see anyone nearby in the press of students, no one I recognized, anyway. Was someone trying to torment me? Bring it.

For the briefest of moments, the crowd parted and my

eyes settled on a porcelain face, brilliant blue eyes, a black fringe of bangs. And then the shift of bodies blocked her from view.

"Ameline." I breathed out her name, Charlotte instantly tense beside me as she scanned the crowd while my mind struggled with what I'd seen. Ameline Benoit, the former next in line for rulership of the Dumont coven and even more evil than Odette herself, the reason I almost lost my vampire Uncle Frank. Ameline with her cold expression and her near-marriage to Quaid.

"You're certain?" A frown crossed her face. "I don't smell her, Sydlynn."

Again the curtain of students parted, revealing the place my enemy had stood. Nothing. Empty. She was gone.

"If she was even ever there." I hugged myself quickly and shook my head, not wanting to doubt my ears or my eyes but trusting Charlotte's sense of smell. Hadn't she practically been raised with Ameline around? If anyone could identify my enemy with one whiff it would be Charlotte. "Could she have masked herself?"

The weregirl shrugged. "It's possible," she said. "Though unlikely. Not from this distance."

I thought about it a moment, remembering when Sassafras, in mortal form, had been kidnapped and

Galleytrot led on a merry chase after him by the brothers Dumont. They'd been able to hide Sassy's scent.

If it was Ameline, why was she showing herself to me? Especially here, at Harvard, the center of the High Council's power? There were so many plain-clothes Enforcers hanging out here, so many witches, all it would take was one slip-up and she'd be caught and most likely burned at the stake for her crimes.

It had to have been my imagination, as much as I hated to admit it. A trick of my eyes, maybe triggered by my new confidence. I wanted to find her, for a rematch of our last fight. I'd played fair but this time...

Screw fair.

I drifted into my fourth class with a little frown on my face, concentration lost on the question. Maybe I should tell Mom? If Ameline was able to make it past the wards on the Yard without anyone's knowledge, she could be anywhere. But what proof did I have, especially since I doubted myself what I saw? No, I'd keep my crazy talk to myself just in case.

The seat I slid into was near the front, but even in my absent-mindedness I knew better than to choose the front row. As the door to the class slammed shut I glanced up, watched a man stride down the lecture theatre stairs, perfect brown suit and crisp yellow tie obviously expensive. I glanced at my class schedule. The instructor was supposed to be Maryanne Courtney, from some small California coven. Not the tall, handsome blonde with the ice blue eyes and angular features I knew all too well. Not that I knew him personally. I just recognized the bloodstock.

"My name is Albert Dumont." He pronounced it Al-*bear*, stressing the last syllable. "Miss Courtney was unable to teach this semester so I was asked to fill in her place for the History of Magic."

Lovely. And yet, maybe I was overreacting. After all, my Santos teacher hadn't said boo either to me or about me. Now that Mia was the leader of the Dumonts, maybe things were better all the way around.

I knew the moment those cold blue eyes met mine not a thing had changed.

"Class," Albert said in his rolling French accent, "we have a celebrity among us."

Everyone groaned. Including me. Here we go again.

"I was planning on beginning with ancient witch history," he said, a smile pulling the signature Dumont mouth wide, white teeth flashing. "But since Sydlynn Hayle is one of my students, perhaps some more recent history would be in order."

He then launched into the most twisted, one sided, non-objective retelling of the Purity coven attack on my family, I had to dig my finger nails into my palms and grit my teeth tightly together to keep from leaping to my feet and tearing him apart.

It was clear from the looks on the other student's faces they were pretty sure he was full of crap, especially when he tried to tell them all my mother was the instigator of the whole thing. My classmates may not have liked me, but they all knew exactly who Miriam Hayle was. And what she'd done to save the High Council.

What I'd done. With Gram's help. Only of course it all was attributed to Mom. Fury bubbled in the pit of my stomach as the brothers snorted and giggled behind me.

Class couldn't be over fast enough. In fact, the door swung open far sooner than I expected, considering the torture I endured. Only, it turned out the session wasn't done. A tall, thin woman in a flowered dress, her bleach blonde curls pulled back in a soft pony tail, stomped down the steps to face off with Albert.

"Class," she said—okay, snarled, long, red painted nails flashing as she pointed at the smiling Dumont, "you will disregard anything this charlatan has told you." She leaned close, growled something at him. He just laughed at her, whispered something back. Her cheeks flamed, body ridged as he drifted out of the room, all eyes on him. Albert winked at me, saluted the brothers and exited with a flourish.

We all turned back to who could only be Maryanne Courtney. I could tell from her long, lean body and deep tan she had to be the very witch meant to teach us.

"I'm sorry about that," she huffed, hands on hips. "And no offense to any other covens, but that man is a douchebag."

I loved her already.

What followed was the most fun I'd ever had in a class. Ever. Maryanne was nothing if not blunt, to the point and full of snarky sarcastic goodness, a fact which colored her teaching to the extent she had the entire student body in the palm of her well-manicured hands.

I was still giggling as I gathered my things to leave when the door swung open, not really wanting to go. For the first time all day I was one of the other students, with no one staring or whispering or treating me like I was different. Maryanne actually waved at me on the way out, but not to single me out. Just to say goodbye.

Awesome.

The only tarnish to the moment was the matching grins from the Dumont brothers as they brushed their way past me, but it was easy enough to forget about them after the great class I'd just sat through.

Not so much for Charlotte, though. She snarled in her Eastern-European language at them, body tense and anger radiating. I found myself grinning and poking her in the side to which she stared at me like I'd done something she'd never for a moment thought anyone would do.

"Helps to think about how they'd look naked," I grinned. Blushed. "Not like that," I corrected. "But, you know. In class. Humiliated." Okay, this was going downhill in a hurry as Charlotte glared at me. "How about dead? Does imagining them dead work for you?"

Now she was smiling, an evil expression. Okay then. Good to know what turned her crank.

I was rather enjoying my new "don't give a flying crap" attitude when someone slid up beside me. My grin was still in place when I turned my head and met Mia's ice blue ones. It took a lot to resist hugging her, I was in that good of a mood.

She smiled back, slow and hesitant, before taking my hand and squeezing it gently. "Hi, Syd."

I squeezed back, but let her go when she pulled away. "Hey, Mia."

Black eyeliner crumpled around the edges of her brilliant eyes as her smile widened. "I've missed you," she whispered before laughing a little. But there was a brittle undercurrent to her amusement reminding me of Alison when my former bestie tried to cover up when something was wrong.

"I missed you too." I really did. She was one of the only friends I'd ever had and somehow being enemies, or at least our covens not really getting along if you could call generations of animosity that, felt like all kinds of wrong. Especially after I'd reconnected with Rupe and Simon just an hour or so ago. "Love you're back to the Goth."

She flushed slightly under her pale makeup, touching her long, black hair. "I feel most comfortable in it," she said. "The most like me. Does that make sense?"

I didn't bother answering, because it kind of did, but not in a good way. I always thought she was hiding the real her behind all that makeup and stainless steel.

"How are things?" I didn't want to prod, but she was just standing there, looking at me as if she expected me to keep the conversation going and it was the only thing I could think of to ask that hopefully wouldn't set her off. Or me. Or make her cry.

Jeeze, talk about complicated.

She shrugged a little, looking away. "Wonderful," she said, that edge still in her voice. "The coven is really coming together under my leadership. I've never been so happy, surrounded by my family."

Um. Okay. Sounded like something she'd come up

with to tell the press, not a casual answer to an equally casual question.

"Good to hear," I said, not wanting to dig any deeper. It really wasn't any of my business. In fact, anything I said outside of the usual could be seen as interfering with another coven.

I was really starting to hate politics.

"Yes," she said so brightly as she turned to meet my eyes again, a wall of falseness between us, "I'm thrilled."

She was totally full of it and I know she knew I saw right through her. But neither of us was in a place to talk about it further and I was pretty sure from the hint of pleading in her expression she wanted me to just nod and smile.

So I did. And her soft sigh of relief told me I'd read her correctly. Whatever was really happening with the Dumont clan, it wasn't anything with which I could interfere. Meaning, no matter how much I cared about Mia, I had to let it go.

I needed to change the subject. The slowly growing discomfort of our silence stretched out so thin I was going to run away if I didn't come up with something to say. When I finally latched onto a bit of news to tell her, I was so relieved I practically pounced on her.

"Blood's here!" My words squealed out of me, far more

excited than I intended. But Mia took the offering and gushed as much as I did.

"He is?" She giggled behind her hands, blue eyes sparkling. "You saw him?"

I nodded quickly. "He doesn't look anything like himself," I said. "Buzz cut, no makeup. But he's the same old Blood." I found myself really laughing. She was the first person who knew him like I did who I could talk to about it, and that fact cut the last of the tension. "Did you know his real name is Rupert?"

Mia giggled again. "I know," she rolled her eyes, black lipsticked lips peeling back from her very white teeth as she smiled. "Silly, right? But he was Blood when I met him."

Mia had this thing, adapting herself like a chameleon to the people she cared about. I wondered why she was Goth again, considering the rest of her family favored the overdone model look and for the first time considered maybe I was wrong about her and it wasn't a way for her to hide after all. If she had enough of a backbone to revert to who she really thought she was, maybe there was hope for her as leader yet.

"I should go to class." She paused, hands clutched together, pressed to her chest. "I just wanted to say hello. And offer a warning."

My entire body tensed. "Warning?" Was she threatening me?

"Stay away from Jean Marc and Kristophe," she said.

Charlotte snarled beside me. I'd forgotten she was there, but as my own anger surged I felt hers push against me.

"Thanks for that," I said, feeling the iciness of my words strike Mia like blows. "You can be certain I will—if they offer the same courtesy."

Mia's eyes flew wide, one hand covering her mouth as her body shuddered. "No, Syd," she whispered. "I'm sorry. That came out all wrong." Her hand dropped, shoulders drooping and guilt replaced my flash of rage. "I just meant... they are holding a grudge against you." Her eyes rimmed with moisture, lips quivering as she fought emotions. "I've ordered them to stay away from you, but I don't trust them to obey."

So that's what being a heel felt like. I reached out to touch her, to apologize, but Mia was already pulling away. "Please be careful," she said. "I can't control them."

I stood there and watched her go, regret at war with frustration. I wished I could fix things between our families, but at the same time I struggled with the fact my friend really wasn't strong enough to lead her coven.

And knew it.

I turned to Charlotte with a frown. "Keep an eye on them," I said, both of us knowing who "they" were. "But stay clear. Okay?"

Her teeth ground together with a squeaking sound. "As you wish. But."

I nodded. "But. If they try anything, we don't hesitate to kill them both."

Charlotte's answering smile could have lit up a room.

The moment I entered the lecture theater, my eyes settled on the Dumont brothers. Great, was I destined to spend every damned class with the pair of irritating fleas? Clearly that was the case. The only thing I could do at this point was ignore them.

As my gaze drifted over the gathering students, I caught sight of another familiar face. The half-smile and wave I began froze in place as Sashenka's eyes flickered away from me. She slunk down in her seat a little, not looking my way at all, though I knew she'd seen me. Lovely, just lovely. Whatever I'd done to make her hate me wasn't going away. And since she obviously didn't want me around, I'd have to do something about our little living arrangement. As much as I hated the thought of defeat, of having to ask Mom to change my roommate, there was no way I was spending the entire year with someone who didn't want me around.

Since Sashenka would prefer I didn't sit with her or even acknowledge I knew her, I slid into a lower row closer to the front, one where no one else was sitting, found the center of it and planted myself with resolve. The new and improved Syd didn't need anyone, thanks. Sashenka Hensley could take a flying leap for all I cared. I had everyone and everything I needed and some second daughter of a coven's shunning of me wasn't about to get me down.

Surprise, surprise, I was alone by the time the main door closed and our teacher strode down to the front of the class. I looked down at my notebook, refusing to let any of this get to me. I was a Hayle, damn it. So what if no one wanted to sit with me? So what if no one liked me? I was a good person, a powerful witch, co-leader of my coven. Yes, I was alone, but I could handle it. All those years of being the odd one out was to strengthen me, to teach me to be self-sufficient. There was no one to come to my rescue. I had to do my own rescuing.

Besides, loneliness was going to come with the territory of being full leader someday. Look at Mom, carrying the weight of the full Council on her shoulders. Not like Dad was around much now that he was a Demon Prince of the Second Plane. And she couldn't very well confide in my little sister. Though I did regret the loss of Sassafras to the pair of them. He would have whipped me into instant shape with a sharp tongue-lashing.

There was always Gram, too. I had her in my head 24/7. My demon. Shaylee. Silly Syd. I was the least alone person I knew.

I could hear the brothers whispering, laughing, but they didn't bother me anymore. In fact, I felt my heart swell open, new confidence rising. I could handle it. More than handle it, I was born for it. I could do anything, had conquered more things in my short eighteen years than those sniping brothers or ungrateful roommate or any other witch in this room had ever endured. Let's see them survive an attack on their coven, being burned at the stake, rescuing a vampire from a virus devouring him, save their mother from certain death.

Yeah, let's just.

The main door swished open then shut again as the teacher turned to face us, his round face looking bored, voice a dull monotone. I ignored the latecomer, basking in my new resolve, soaking up my internal power until my demon hummed in happiness and Shaylee preened at how amazing we all were. I was well aware this was only a tactic, a protection mechanism, but I needed it right now and wasn't about to turn away the tools I had on hand to survive.

Whoever joined us late took a seat right next to me.

I steadfastly refused to turn my head, keeping myself to myself, a little rigid, hoping the other witch would just back off. After all, the whole row was empty. Did he have to sit next to me?

It was a he, I could tell from the size of his knees out of the corner of my eye, catching sight of the faded denim of his jeans. There was a familiar aroma about him, a mix of earth and fabric softener. But it wasn't until his hand reached over and touched mine that I gasped and understood.

Green magic snaked between us, the surge of Sidhe power drawing my head around. Liam smiled at me, his hazel eyes sparkling with green flecks as he bent forward so we were gaze-to-gaze.

"Hey, Syd," he whispered. "What did I miss?"

Okay, so all of that "I can do it on my own, I'm amazing" crap? Yeah, well, that all went out the window the moment I looked into Liam's eyes. My throat tightened instantly as I grasped his hand and found myself beaming at him.

"Hey, Liam," I whispered back, whole body vibrating with the sudden surge of joy I felt at seeing him again. "Not much."

Yes, it had only been a day or so since we parted ways, but for some reason it felt like forever. It was only then I understood how much I relied on my Gatekeeper friend, how much his friendship meant to me. Liam was my rock, my utterly loyal and unjudgmental rock who didn't care what I did or how I looked or acted. He loved me anyway.

I wanted to hug him, to squeal in happiness and hang onto him, but the teacher, Walden Bradford, was glaring so I was forced to sit back and face the front of the room, though it was impossible to wipe the grin from my face and there was no way I was letting Liam's hand go.

He didn't fight me so I figured he was as happy to see me as I was to see him.

Walden droned on and on for what felt like hours about the world of Witchcraft, all the monsters, creatures and different families and types of magic we'd be learning about this year. He might as well have been reciting the phone book for all I paid attention. By the time he was done and the door swung open, I was so wound up I spun in my chair and hugged Liam where he sat. He laughed into my hair, hugging me back, the warmth and earthiness making everything all right again. We sat there while the rest of the students piled out, grinning at each other like idiots.

"What are you doing here?" I punched his knee with my free hand. "I thought you had to stay and guard the Gate?" Liam's family had been responsible for guarding over the Sidhe gate in Wilding Springs for generations. And since he was the last O'Dane, his was a very important job. Without him, when the yearly knock of the Sidhe came to call, without a Gatekeeper to answer it, the whole of both of the Seelie and Unseelie courts would be free to return to our world.

We'd had a taste of that already and I wasn't really ready for another.

Liam shrugged, a long, slow motion rippling over his wide shoulders and making his white t-shirt bunch over his chest. "Ethpeal and Miriam convinced me to come to school," he said in his deep voice. I'd missed that voice. "I've known for a few weeks, but I really wanted to surprise you." His teeth flashed against his tanned skin, so much good humor in his eyes I couldn't be angry with him for not keeping me in the know. "It was so hard to keep the secret."

I jabbed him with the point of my pen before relenting. "So you left Galleytrot on guard? But didn't we test trying to go into the cavern without you and no luck?"

An experiment from the summer, to see if it would accept anyone else. Didn't like me, apparently. Galleytrot either, at least at the time. Which meant Liam was stuck.

Had been.

Liam nodded. "We weren't sure it would work," he said. "I infused him with some of my magic. It didn't want to go to him, I'll tell you." He shuddered. "Felt like I was leaving part of myself behind. But we both adapted. And so far, it's worth it." Hazel eyes warmed further, drawing me in.

Liam was here. How cool was that?

"Galleytrot can let me know if anything happens," he went on. "Besides, the knock already came this year, so there's not much to do besides study." Liam tapped his books with one big hand. "And I can do that here. Besides, I have this friend? She can get me home pretty quick if I need to go."

He sure did.

I finally gained my feet, Liam towering over me like a tall, young oak tree. Everything about him reminded me of spring and growing things and the earth. I waited until we'd cleared the seats before turning and hugging him as hard as I could, my nose pressed to the delicious scent of his shirt. Liam hugged me back, cheek resting on my hair and I couldn't help but sigh in happiness.

I opened my eyes, unable to censor the happy smile on my face, only to spot Quaid watching us.

Quaid! My body took over, leaping away from Liam and surging toward his dark yumminess, nothing else even crossing my mind but to get to him and feel his body against me. I wrapped my arms around his neck, hands sliding into his hair as I pulled him tightly to me and pressed my lips into his ear.

"Quaid," I whispered, feeling his body shudder as my breath trailed over his skin. But he didn't hug me back, holding himself stiff until I pulled away, happiness fading as I leaned back and looked up into his eyes. Was he okay?

Had something happened? My concern, fear even, was met with something I hadn't expected, but should have.

He wasn't looking at me. Nope. Quaid instead glared right at Liam. And my handsome Sidhe friend stared right back.

Oh, just flipping wonderful. I jerked free of the delicious guy I was in love with and snapped my fingers in front of his nose, forcing him to break his stare and meet my eyes. Dark, almost black, they flashed with jealousy, so much my anger surged to replace the joy I'd felt at finally seeing him again. Even my demon, usually uncontrollable when it came to him, snarled in anger.

"Nice," I snapped at him. "I haven't seen you in months, you avoid me ever since you get here and when we finally get to see each other, what do you do? Pull the jealous card." I spun to point at Liam. "As it happens, I've been alone since I arrived. Get me?" I pushed against Quaid's hard stomach, feeling how tense he still was. "Liam just got here too. So you can read anything you want into what you just saw, but you can do it without my input."

Liam's voice rumbled from deep inside him as he spoke, hazel eyes more green than ever, flashing Sidhe fire, whole body tense and threatening. "At least someone was here for her."

I turned to storm off, but my anger wouldn't let me just yet. "And you," I shot at Liam. "Get a freaking grip already. Quaid isn't out to hurt me, so you can drop the Mr. Protective act. I'm quite capable of taking care of myself."

Liam looked away, broad shoulders slumping. "Sorry, Syd."

But Quaid didn't say anything, not one word, his smoldering gaze locked on me as if he blamed me for something. The hell he did. No way was he judging me, not when he abandoned me the way he had. Not when my friend seemed to care about me more than my so-called boyfriend. Here I was, anticipating seeing him for what felt like forever, with only emails, Skype and the occasional mental connection to keep me going and what does he do? Does his best to avoid me, or so it felt like and then when he finally showed up turns into a total jerk.

Not the sweet reunion I'd been hoping for.

"Grow up, Quaid" I snapped. "When you finally find time to come say hi without being a jerk, you know where to find me. I may or may not be there."

Zing. Okay, done. I turned and marched off, head high, Charlotte right behind me, leaving the two of them to work it out. I was so done with the pair of them not getting along.

Sadness tried to creep in, but I wasn't having any. I'd waited all freaking summer to see Quaid. We'd been through so much in the last two years, were pushed to our limits, both of us, finally having the chance to be together. And hadn't he left me? Yeah. A bunch of times. Maybe it was time for me to reconsider my boyfriend choice.

Not even my pissed-off demon was buying that one as my heart contracted at the very thought. This incredible pull I felt for him, as though the fates themselves had locked us together, simply wouldn't let me go. And even as I stomped off in a hissy fit, my soul begged me for Quaid.

Stupid fates. They could kiss my behind.

I stormed out the magicked door and into the main lobby of the library. Where to go? I couldn't go to my room, not yet. Not to Sashenka. Like I needed more problems. And going there meant Quaid would have an easier time finding me. Nope. He'd have to work for it, damn him. Instead, I followed a flow of students moving deeper into the library, hoping for a quiet corner and some time to stew.

Instead, I spotted two faces sitting at a near-by table and headed their way, hoping some time with Rupe and Simon would take my mind off the mess of my life.

"Hey, Syd." Rupe's grin was more welcome than seeing Liam or Quaid, without an agenda, just normal. I smiled back and sat with them, letting my bag thud to the tabletop.

"Hey, guys." I sat back, arms crossed over my chest. "Hope you two had a better first day than I did."

Simon's steady blinking was mesmerizing and kind of gave me a twitch. But he was my friend and had always been quirky so I let it go.

"Had a great day." Simon patted his calculus book with the arrogant smile I didn't like. "Piece of cake."

Rupe rolled his eyes. "Yeah, well, I think Simon will be tutoring me all year, but it'll be okay."

Simon snorted softly. "If I have time," he said, eyebrows arching as if he was better than us all of a sudden. What the hell happened to my sweet young friend? Darin's face popped into my head and I found myself fighting a scowl.

"Something keeping you busy?" If Simon was involved with witches, it couldn't be for good reasons. I was keenly aware my friend could be getting himself into something he just wouldn't be able to handle. And while I didn't know Darin personally, I knew the type.

The Dumont type. I'd have to check into his family's loyalties and see if he was from a line of trouble or just a single troublemaker.

"I'm working on some things," Simon said before hunching down with a grin telling me the guy I cared about was still safe and sound inside him. "It's so cool, you guys."

Rupe jabbed him gently while I dropped my arms and leaned in. "Spill it, kiddo."

I really wanted him to, but I was glad Rupe did the asking. Yes, Simon was normal, but I couldn't be seen to be interfering with another coven.

"You know there aren't any fraternities here, right?" Simon looked back and forth between us like it was some big secret.

"That's right," Rupe said. "Harvard doesn't allow them."

"But there are clubs," Simon said. "Final clubs they're called. And my friend Darin is part of one." Simon sat back with a big grin, like he was the king of the world. "The Star Club. And he's invited me to join."

Huge warning bells went off in my head. There's no way someone like Simon would be invited to a Final Club. For one, his family wasn't rich. He was here on a full scholarship because he was brilliant. And besides, if Darin was a member, it's likely the club was only for witches. Star Club. Pentagram. Yeah, how freaking obvious could they get?

Rupe seemed impressed, though. "Cool," he said. "Think I could join? Be a great way to meet people."

Simon's lip turned up into a tiny sneer. "Maybe," he said. "I'll talk to Darin to see if you have the right material to be a Star."

So this was what was turning Simon into a jerk. The idea he was special. What kind of bull was Darin shoveling into him to make him act like this way? I shuddered as I thought about it. I'd spent my whole life wanting to be normal. But for a boy like him, growing up brilliant but nerdy, never fitting in anywhere, the idea he could stand out, be part of something like a Final Club, no matter the cost to his ego or what he had to do to get in… I had to look in to this further.

"Wow, a club." I found myself grinning. "Do they have a secret handshake?"

Simon's sneer faded. "What?"

I winked at Rupe. "How about a decoder ring? A decoder ring would be way cool." If only I could get Simon to realize what he was involved in, to laugh about it a little. Even if Darin and the Star Club were legit, Simon was a genius and wonderful just the way he was. Anyone who wanted to convert him into a jerk wasn't okay in my books.

My attempt to make him poke fun at himself and his new friends fell, shall we say, very flat. Instead of finding it funny, his face scrunched into an angry scowl.

"You have no idea who you are mocking," he snarled. "The Star Club is the elite of the elite and you're just jealous they want me." Simon stood, grasping his books to his skinny chest before stalking off in a snit.

I met Rupe's eyes, feeling suddenly sick and wishing I'd gone about it in another way. "Am I the only one who's worried about him?"

Rupe's gaze followed Simon before returning to me. "No," he said at last. "Darin's got him wrapped up, I saw that much. But who are we to tell Simon what he can't do?"

I nodded, glum and feeling like I'd stumbled from one disaster to another all day. If only I could crawl under the covers and forget any of this happened. But Sashenka was likely back in our room and I just couldn't bring myself to face her.

My eyes caught movement across the library and I spotted a familiar face. I was suddenly on my feet, waving and grinning to Mia who drifted over, her black-rimmed eyes locked on Rupe.

He stood, turning to her, a slow smile spreading over his face. Neither said a word as he opened his arms and Mia stepped into them.

Clearly no longer welcome, I turned, grinning my face off, and left them to get reacquainted, feeling at last like something had gone right.

I had no choice. I had to go to my room eventually. With Charlotte ever my silent bodyguard, I drifted across the Yard toward the dorm, walking slower and slower with each step as dread tried to keep me from finishing the trip.

"Miss Hayle." I turned, grateful for the distraction, to face a smiling young man in a crisp black uniform. I recognized him, though couldn't place from where. It wasn't until he handed me a sheet of paper the same color as his outfit, reddish curls as round as his cheeks, that I made the connection.

"You're her page." One of them. I knew him from the trial. He'd stood with Maurice, now Mom's secretary and a second page.

"Vincent." He winked at me. I found myself grinning even though he might have been fourteen, but was clearly flirting. "We never actually met, coven leader."

I took the paper from him. "I guess we didn't," I said. "I was too busy trying to save Mom."

He bobbed a nod. "Leadership looks great on you." Another wink. Really? Smart ass. But at least he was adorable enough it made up for his cheekiness.

One look at the sheet made my stomach clench. It was an invitation to dinner. An official invitation. Now, don't get me wrong. I was totally okay with invites to things, especially anything requiring such an invitation. But not when I was being summoned to dine with my mother. Clearly written by her secretary. And stamped with her magical seal.

Teeth suddenly on edge, annoyance my own mother would send an errand boy to fetch me with some tacky magical invite in his greasy little hand, I reached out with my power, despite knowing it was bad form, and touched Mom's magic.

You could have just asked. I was terrible at keeping anger out of my voice when I spoke out loud, but even worse at it using mental communication. Something about the closeness of the touch of power made everything bigger and more obvious.

Mom's sigh wasn't lost on me. *It's your first official dinner with me*, she sent. *Can you at least allow me to treat you like you're special?*

Like that's what it was about. *Sure, fine. See you*, I glanced at the time on the invitation then at my watch, *in about two minutes*. Way to give me any kind of advanced notice.

Mom let me go, feeling as irritated as I did. Lovely. This could be one of those times I'd be better off just going back to my room after all. But instead I crammed the black sheet into the front pocket of my jean skirt and, ignoring Vincent, stomped off with my backpack digging into my shoulder toward Massachusetts Hall and my mother.

The university president's office was in the same building as Mom's. But I wasn't sure if said president was aware of the invisible top floor only accessible from inside the building. I rode an old-fashioned elevator, well-disguised from normal eyes, all the way to the top and Mom's private quarters.

My bad mood dissolved the second the doors creaked open and my little sister bounced through to hug me.

"Syd!" Meira's right horn dug into my shoulder as she squeezed me as hard as she could. I hugged her back, ignoring the jab, just happy to see a smiling face.

Her cheeks were pinker than usual despite her red-toned skin and her teeth flashed white against her deeper lips as she looked up into my eyes. She'd grown since I saw her in June, at least two inches taller, face more mature. How had I missed she was growing up? The knowledge made me sad we'd been apart over the summer, not to mention I suddenly felt old.

My demon wrapped her power around Meira, Shaylee welcoming her too before my sister finally pulled away, still holding my hand as she half-pulled me forward through the dark wood paneled entry and into a big, open sitting area. I turned, caught sight of Charlotte stopped in the doorway.

"I can't pass," she said. The scowl on her face told me volumes.

Meira paused, bit her lower lip. "Sorry, Charlotte," she said. "Mom will have to clear you." Her amber eyes met mine. "She had to do it for me and Sass, too."

Charlotte nodded brusquely. "Very well," she said. "I'll wait here." Yeah, she was happy about it, too. I left my backpack with her and followed Meira.

Thing is, I would have liked to have stayed with my bodywere. The sitting room, the whole upper floor, in fact, felt oppressive despite the tall ceilings, thanks to more dark wood and the tall, grim paintings of previous High Council leaders lining the walls. Their creepy eyes seemed to follow me as Meira dragged me through the sitting room and toward a large, heavily carved door. A wide, long table of more of the dark wood sat in the middle of the next room, covered in black linens and china with silver and gold leaf edges.

"Isn't it awesome here?" Meira sank into a chair, still grinning, as I took the one beside her. I glanced around, looking for Mom, not really surprised she wasn't in sight, though I could feel her moving toward us.

"You're liking it?" I focused on my sister and found myself smiling. "You look great, Meems. I missed you a lot."

No way was I crying. But Meira had her own tears in her eyes as she leaned in and hugged me again. "Me too," she said before pulling back. "But I really do like it here, Syd." Her old happy smile wreathed her face. "I get to go to witch school. It's amazing." Her cute nose wrinkled as she helped herself to the glass of water in front of her plate. Obviously eating here in this big room at a table that would easily seat thirty didn't faze her any. "So much better than any normal school."

"You don't have to hide." I leaned forward and kissed her forehead. She swatted at me, but beamed as she held my gaze.

"Exactly." She sighed happily. "There are a few Dumont kids here, but no one listens to them anymore." Meira's smile deepened. "Those girls who were mean to me at camp? Yeah, nobody likes them. But they do like me."

"Naturally." A large ball of silver fur landed on the end of the table. Sassafras sauntered down the center of it as if he owned the place, weaving in around goblets and table wear until he came to a halt before me. "What's not to love?" He sat, tail flipping forward to wrap around him as he observed me with his half-lidded amber eyes. "Unlike Sydlynn, here."

There was no way I could resist. I leaned forward and gathered him into my arms, snuggling him against my chest, pressing my face into his soft fur, breathing in the lovely cat scent of him reminding me of newborn kittens and crackling winter fires.

"Sass," I whispered. "I missed you."

His paws settled on my shoulders as I let him lean back, nose coming forward to press to mine as he started to purr. "Silly girl," he said, voice thick though I knew he'd deny any such emotional reaction later, "of course you did."

My laugh bubbled up, taking me over as I snuggled him close again. "Oh Sassy," I said in my best little girl voice, "you're my favorite kitty, ever."

Meira giggled while Sass's tail thrashed, a deep growl coming from his chest.

"Honestly, Sydlynn," he hissed. "Will you never grow up?"

I let him go, giggling with my sister. "I hope not."

"Me either," she said.

Sassy snorted and began licking one paw with great vigor. "It's a curse, I tell you," he said, "being saddled with you Hayle witches."

Somehow that made us laugh harder.

We were still laughing when a door at the end of the room swung open and Mom strode in. My good humor faded as she approached, not looking at us, head down and to the side, listening to her secretary as he whispered in her ear. I'd never gotten along with Maurice and always had the impression he saw me as a bother, a nuisance in the way of Mom's complete attention.

When Mom finally looked up, her blue eyes found mine. "Sydlynn."

I stood slowly as she came to my side. "Mom."

Our hug was strained and it bothered me. A lot. But it was hard to commit to her when I felt her unwilling to do the same, especially with Maurice hovering behind her, glaring like I was taking up precious time better spent elsewhere.

Mom hugged Meira with more enthusiasm and even bent to kiss Sassafras on the head.

"Charlotte can't enter." It came out a little harsher than

I meant it and from the frown Mom shot me she didn't appreciate my tone.

"I'll make sure she's on the list." Mom took a seat, pulled out and shoved back in by Vincent who magically appeared at her side.

"Miriam, we must discuss tomorrow's meeting." Maurice ignored the rest of us. "I'm certain the Dumont contingent will raise the same issues as last time."

It took a lot for me not to sigh as the interruptions of our family time continued through the entire meal. A very fast, very tense meal. By the time I was served my main course, I was ready to stab Maurice through the eye with my fork. Mom was just as bad, spending half her time in silent communication with the Council. My frustration hit overload when I caught the unhappy look on Meira's face and the way Sassafras's whiskers drooped as he backed away from his half-finished meal.

"Isn't this nice?" Oh Syd, when will you learn to keep your mouth shut? But I just couldn't sit there and live this lie any longer. "Our happy family, spending happy family time over dinner together."

Mom shot me a look half-angry, half-guilty while Maurice sighed in a heavy huff.

"Maurice," Mom said. "Please excuse us, will you?"

He stared at her like she'd asked him to commit suicide. "Council Leader?"

Mom stared at me, face calm and quiet. Had I gotten through to her? "Just go."

He wavered, hesitated, as though Mom might change her mind, offer him some reprieve. When she ignored him he left, clearly upset with the state of affairs.

"I'm sorry," Mom said. "You're very right, Syd. This is family time."

Well. What do you know? "It's good to see you, Mom." I meant it. She looked great. A little tired around the eyes, but if Maurice was any indicator, it's not likely she was getting much rest.

"You too, sweetheart." She softened instantly and suddenly she was my mom again. "How was your first day?"

Yeah, didn't want to talk about that. "Thanks for encouraging Liam to come to school." I toyed with my pasta, thinking about Quaid and the mess I'd left behind earlier.

"He's an excellent student," Mom said, "and while he's tied to the Gate, he can be a great asset to the Council in the times he's not fulfilling that capacity."

Really? Was he just a tool to her? My anger returned, even when Sassy flashed me a glare from his amber eyes and changed the subject.

But no matter what we talked about, Mom turned it back into something about work. Work, work, always her work until I felt like Maurice might have well stuck around.

He gave us maybe ten minutes as it was, appearing through the door again to hover at Mom's elbow before I even had a chance to sniff at the dessert Vincent set before me.

I was about to totally lose it when Erica rushed in and came right to my side. She hugged me while I was still in the chair, her long, blonde hair falling over my shoulder. Mom's second in command was now the Hayle member of the Council and the change had done her good. Always in Mom's shadow, Erica Plower had blossomed. She looked fantastic and her genuine kindness and happiness when she pulled away from me was a far cry from the troubled and fearful woman who had tried to wrest control of the family from me when Mom was on trial.

"Syd," she said, "it's so good to see you!"

Erica slid around the table, taking a seat across from me, smiling at Vincent who set her own dessert in front of her.

"You too, Erica." She'd arrived just in time to diffuse my ticking bomb and I was grateful. I really didn't want to fight with Mom, but if this was going to be the extent of our relationship from now on, I wasn't sure I could keep my temper in check.

"Sorry I'm late, I wanted to be here earlier, but Council business calls." She smiled at Mom, at Meira, at Sassafras. "How was first day?"

I wasn't going there, not when she seemed so happy. But I did have one thing I had to deal with. "Things are great," I said. "But I do have something I need to deal with."

Mom's forehead bunched as she frowned a little. "What's wrong?"

"Sashenka." I set down my fork as my stomach clenched. "She's Tallah Hensley's sister?"

"Your roommate." Mom nodded. "I made sure the two of you were together. Since you seemed to get along well when you met."

"Well, I'm not sure what I did to piss her off," I said, "but she can't stand me now." I hated admitting it, with Maurice and Vincent watching, even Erica. But there was no telling when I'd have a chance to talk to Mom again. "I'll be needing a new roommate."

Mom looked like she wanted to argue but sighed finally, sitting back like I really was at fault. "Fine then. But you have to share with someone, even if it's Charlotte."

Great attitude, Mom. Way to be on my side. "I didn't say I wanted special treatment," I said through teeth not quite clenched but close. "But I can't live with someone who won't even talk to me."

"Just give her another chance, Syd." Erica looked back and forth between me and Mom, face creased in concern. "I'm sure it's probably nothing."

Leave it to Erica to side with Mom. Shocker.

"I'm not sure what you expect to change," I said, "but whatever. I'll give it until the end of the week. This isn't my choice, Mom. It's Sashenka's."

As much as I didn't want to be different, to have special treatment, I would have taken a room on my own in a heartbeat.

12

Maurice brought out a large book, flipped it open, one finger poised over a black sheet. "Shall we schedule dinners on Sundays from now on, Council Leader? For efficiency's sake."

Mom almost flinched but nodded. "Yes, thank you."

"Six pm, shall we?" He wrote quickly, magic flowing from his finger to the page as he decided my once-a-week culinary fate for the rest of the year in his stupid appointment book. "Now then," Maurice snapped the book shut, turning to face Mom with a no-nonsense look on his face, "we have business, Council Leader."

Mom rose, set aside her black napkin. "Yes, of course." She paused, eyes meeting mine. I let her see how angry I was, saw her own frustration rise. "Good night, Sydlynn."

"Yeah," I shot back as she turned away, "nice to see you too, Mom."

She left without another word, Maurice rushing her out as Vincent rushed forward and began to clear the table with brief surges of air magic winging the plates and cutlery out from under us.

I threw down my own napkin, surging to my feet, wanting to go after Mom, to shake her and ask her what the hell was wrong with her. But Meira sat there, looking sad and hurt and I couldn't just abandon my sister like Mom clearly had.

I hugged Meira as she rose. "Love you, Meems."

"Love you too, Syd." She snuffled a little, pulled free. "Did you want to come see my room?"

I followed her to the grandiose, high ceilinged monstrosity she slept in and did my best to murmur appreciation for the dark wood theme that continued throughout, the heavy, elaborate bed reminding me of some Gothic boudoir and the overall feeling of oppression I had from the place.

Not my first choice for a comfy and happy sleeping arrangement, but Meira seemed content so I let it go.

After a tense few minutes talking where I could hardly focus on a word she said, my sister sighed. "Guess I should go do my homework."

I was as bad as Mom. This wasn't Meira's fault. I should be supporting her, not wrapping myself up in my own crap. "I'm sorry, sis."

Meira shrugged. "It's not always like this," she said as

Sassafras leaped up beside me on the bed and set one silver paw on her hand where she perched next to me, amber eyes glowing in sympathy. "But mostly."

"I promise I'll come over and visit a lot." I hugged her again, one hand stroking Sassy's fur. "Okay?"

Meira nodded into my shirt. "Kay."

It was hard to leave, but I did. I was in no state of mind to hang with my sister anyway. I'd likely start griping about Mom and Meira didn't need to hear what was spinning around in my head. Hell, I didn't want to hear it but couldn't make it stop.

I turned my back on Erica when she tried to follow me out, gathering up the angry Charlotte and hitting the down button on the elevator. Erica backed off, face sad and just stood and watched as the doors closed on us.

"I'm guessing that went well." Charlotte's voice echoed with a touch of her wereness.

"You have no idea." I sighed and leaned against the wall as we descended, my dinner sitting unhappily in my stomach. "Be grateful you couldn't come in. Trust me."

It was a short walk from Massachusetts Hall to the dorm, but my feet dragged. My backpack felt like it weighed a million pounds, about as heavy as my heart. I was so wrapped up in feeling sorry for myself and being angry with Mom I almost missed the feeling of someone brushing up against me. I glanced to my left, frowning, Charlotte tense on my right.

"What is it?" She looked around, nostrils flaring.

"You felt that?" I had a good idea I knew the source of the contact, but wanted confirmation from my wereguard before I did anything drastic.

"We're not alone." The Yard was pretty much empty, but I knew what she meant.

I stopped, drew my shields in tight and even spun them out to protect Charlotte. "Alison," I said. "What do you want?"

"You know what I want." My ex-bestie appeared next to me, floating in thin air, eyes sunken, blonde hair rippling in a non-existent breeze.

"You can't have it." She was still fixated on the virus. I felt it suddenly, vibrating against my skin. I had to deal with her, but how? I just couldn't bring myself to destroy the last bit of my friend remaining. I knew I'd regret it eventually, but after the day I'd had there was no way I was adding best friend murderer to the list of crap I'd endured.

"I'll be real again, if you just give it to me." White fire burned in Alison's eyes, the touch of the virus she'd already stolen more than enough to keep her here on this plane, longing for more. "We could be together, you and me, Al and Syd." She blinked at me, all innocent. "Don't you want that?"

Sadness washed away the last of the anger at Mom. As much as I wanted my friend back, I knew this would only end in disaster. And no one else was going to take care of this for me. I had to release Alison, send her on. It was the only way she would have peace.

"Al," I whispered. "I'm sorry things turned out this way. Please always know I love you." Without warning, I reached out with my spirit magic like Gram had taught me and banished her back across to death.

She shimmered like a candle flame threatening to go out, mouth open in a large 'O' of denial before she solidified once again.

That wasn't supposed to happen.

I was too shocked I'd failed to do anything when Alison's anger rose, terrible and twisted, turning her once-beautiful face into a monster's mask. "YOU DARE!" She swelled and grew, body distorting like a balloon filled to far, the white light in her eyes bright pin points like stars burning through me. "I THOUGHT YOU LOVED ME!" Her howl tore at my soul, made me clamp my hands over my ears though it did nothing to save me. This wasn't a human sound, but one of the spirit, aimed directly at me.

Charlotte whimpered, shook her head as she caught the edges of the sonic attack, but was helpless against Alison. The echo of my friend rose from the ground, soaring above me as I struggled to come up with something to stop her.

"She told me you'd try to kill me." Alison's voice emerged in a hiss, a knife-blade compared to the hammer of sound she'd just ended. "I should have believed her. And now I do."

A small group of normal students emerged from one of the dorms and headed toward us, laughing and talking. I reached out with my power to snag and capture Alison before they could come closer, but she was quicker than me, diving out of my grasp and flying right into their faces.

They shrieked and scattered, the four girls clearly able to see my friend. Alison vanished in a rush of white light, leaving me to comfort the normal girl who ran right into me, sobbing in terror.

It took a few minutes to calm the girl down, time enough for her friends to come collect her. By the time they all scampered off, now laughing at their obvious confusion and blaming it on some prank thanks to the memory soothing power of the campus magic, I was in no more of a mood to go back to my dorm than I had been before.

So when I spotted Rupe and Simon sneaking across the

Yard, looking very guilty and arousing my suspicions about where they were going by the way they peeked over their shoulders and kept to the shadows of the trees, I couldn't resist following.

13

Before I could take even one step Charlotte had her hand on my arm and pulled me back.

"Just where do you think you're going?" Her voice had taken on the soft growl of her were side. Only then did I realize she'd been through as much as I had today. Left her pack behind, forced to follow me around, she must have been just as frustrated as I felt.

"The secret society thing, remember?" She'd been there, overheard, I was sure of it. "The Star Club. It's for witches." Okay, I was guessing, filling in blanks. "And if Darin is involved, it can't be good." Again, guessing. But from the troubled look on Charlotte's face, she felt the same way I did.

"We'll see where they go," Charlotte said, releasing my arm. "But that's all."

Whatever. "Come on, we'll lose them."

I wished I had time to stow my backpack, but instead was forced to lug it along, the weight bouncing on my back as Charlotte and I jogged across the Yard and toward Widener

Library. I caught sight of the boys passing through between the main building and the smaller side libraries on their way to the street. We reached the busy Massachusetts Avenue just as the pair disappeared down a side street, Holyoke.

I dodged across with Charlotte at my back, slowing as we reached Holyoke. I was just in time, hidden in a patch of shadow, to see my friends climb a narrow set of stairs to a dark painted door and ring the bell. The door opened and the two stepped inside, the portal thudding solidly shut behind them.

I stood there for a long time, looking up at the tall, narrow building sandwiched in between two others of brick.

"Planning to knock?" Charlotte's soft whisper still held humor, but her amusement was as dark as the night sky.

"Likely." I found myself hesitating further. It was tempting to go check the place out, but a few things held me back. I didn't feel any kind of thrall on Simon or Rupe, so Darin wasn't breaking any witch laws. And if he was willing to let two normals into his Club, who was I to say things were hinky? For all I knew, Darin was just planning some prank against them. Or making them do stupid stuff like I'd heard about fraternities. Just because Darin was a creepy jerk with girl issues didn't mean he was planning to hurt my friends.

This really wasn't any of my business. Why then did I feel so nervous?

"Let's go," I said. With no excuse to check in on Simon and Rupe, and unable to interfere with other witches, I had no other choice. "But we'll keep an eye on the Star Club. And my friends."

The return to my dorm felt like a retreat. I hated backing down.

At least my room was empty when I returned. Or mostly. A pile of silver fur with burning amber eyes lay on my pillow, pink nose shiny in the light when I turned it on.

Just the sight of Sassafras sitting there, waiting for me, made tears rise in my eyes. I hurried forward, falling onto the bed to bury my face in his fur, feel the roughness of his tongue on my cheek as he purred in my ear, whole body vibrating with it.

"I've chosen to stay with you for a time," he said softly. "It's quieter here. Not as much Council running about."

"What about Meems?" I wanted to be selfish, but the thought of my little sister all alone broke my heart.

"She has friends over all the time," he said. "Noisy little things, chattering into the night. I could use the rest."

I hugged him, scratching his cheeks, his ears while he rolled over on his back to let me rub his tummy.

"Thanks," I whispered, a single tear falling to sparkle on his fur.

"I missed you too," he said. "And I know how hard this is. How lonely. I don't want you to feel like we've all abandoned you."

I stroked the teardrop from his silky coat. "You're the best, Sass."

He flipped over and head-butted my cheek. "I know," he said. "Now, don't you have some homework or some such to attend to? You're disturbing my nap."

It was so hard not to squeal and squeeze him as punishment, but I resisted.

Barely.

One thing about not being alone anymore, it convinced me I needed to do something about Sashenka. After a brief discussion with Sassafras, it was apparent I wouldn't get anywhere if I didn't know why she hated me in the first place.

"Grow a spine," he said with his personal brand of subtlety. "If you want to know something, ask already."

Okay then. The moment the door creaked open, Sashenka's nervous face peeking through, I was ready for her.

"We need to talk." She flinched at my words, but entered, head down, book bag falling to the floor at her feet with a thud as she pushed the door shut behind her.

"I know," she whispered. "I'm sorry."

"For not liking me?" I shrugged, going for couldn't-care-less casual. "Whatever. But won't room with you if you can't even be civil."

Sashenka's eyes flew wide and she opened her mouth

to speak, a few consonants stuttering out, but I cut her off.

"I have no idea what I did to piss you off," I said, "and frankly, at this point, I don't really care. I thought we were kind of friends, but if Tallah or my mother pushed you into something you really didn't want to do, I understand." I rolled my eyes and sighed. "Believe me, I understand. Welcome to my life."

Sashenka just stood there, trembling, tears standing in her eyes. It took a great deal of effort not to walk up to her and shake her out of whatever kept her frozen.

I think you've underestimated your effect on her. Sassy's mental voice had a softness to it I rarely heard. *I don't think it's that she doesn't like you, Syd.*

I shoved his thoughts aside and went on. "If you want a new roommate, fine. I've already talked to Mom about it. She wants me to give it one more try, but it's pretty obvious where this is going. So I'll tell her in the morning. Unless you want me out tonight." It pissed me off, the thought I'd be the one to leave. But I'd take it. At least I could go stay with Charlotte for one night. Or, heaven forbid, my mother.

Instead of answering, Sashenka threw herself on her bed and burst into sobs.

What?

All my anger melted away, taken over by confusion and a little guilt. "What did I say?"

Sashenka was sobbing so hard while she tried to talk I couldn't understand her words. Probably wouldn't have been able to even if her face wasn't shoved into her pillow, she was so hysterical. Sassafras hopped down and padded his way to her, leaping up with a soft grunt to purr in her ear. Sashenka finally rolled over and hugged him while he cleaned her wet cheeks with his tongue. Part of me felt a jab of jealousy. He was my cat, damn it. The rest of me was just glad my friend was able to calm the girl down before she imploded.

"I'm s-s-sorry," she stuttered around choking gasps of air. "I'm trying so hard, Tallah said this was really important and I really do like you, I've liked you since we met and Tallah does too, but she said I had to try hard to make you like me and I r-r-ruined it all." Her final word trailed off into a wail of despair, the l's lingering long after she pressed her face into Sassy's fur and wept.

Oh boy. So I'd mistaken dislike and avoidance for... well. I perched on the edge of her bed and rubbed her back, feeling like a horrible person for judging her the way I had. "I'm the one who's sorry," I said. "I thought you hated me."

Sashenka shook her head violently. "Ever since you shared your magic with me," she sniffled, "I've wanted to be your friend."

I'd slipped up, the day Mom's trial started, shared magic with her when I was only supposed to with her leader sister, Tallah. "I felt the same way," I said. "I was hoping we could be friends. I've never really had a witch friend before." Pathetic.

Sashenka sat up, Sassy in her lap, his steady purr an undercurrent to our talk. I knew his purr had calming properties, but now I understood how devious he could be. A thread of demon magic ran through it, cooling her down, helping her focus even as she was compelled to stroke his fur over and over.

Tricky little furball. How often had he used that trick on me and I'd never known?

One amber eye winked at me.

"I just wanted everything to be perfect," Sashenka said, oblivious to what my cat was doing to her. "But every time I tried to talk to you, I froze up." She shook her head, refusing to look at me, black hair falling over her dark cheek. "I'm such an idiot."

"No," I said. "You're not. I am. I should have known they put pressure on you."

She finally glanced up, a little smile on her face. "The pressure is all mine," she said. "I've always tried too hard. Comes from being second sister in a leading family. Or so Tallah tells me."

Huh. I immediately thought of Meira. Did my little sister feel the same way? Did she try too hard to fit in because she knew she'd never lead her own coven?

"You're just so powerful," Sashenka let out in a huff of breath. "Everyone is afraid of you, of what you've done, what you can do. And your family." Her deep brown eyes locked on mine, full of so much open honesty I knew I was finally seeing the real Sashenka. "I just didn't want to mess up. I know you can't have many friends, being who you are. I've watched you all day, in class. How they treat you." She hiccupped softly. "I wanted to reach out, but you looked so strong, like you didn't need anyone…"

Yeah, way to be all brave and stuff, Syd.

I felt laughter rising inside me and couldn't stop it. "You have no idea."

Sashenka wiped her nose on the sleeve of her shirt, forehead pinched in concern. "What do you mean?"

I could have backed off, just said screw it. The poor girl had been through enough already, hadn't she? She didn't need me to unload all of my crap on her.

Yes, Sassafras sent, tail flicking. *She does.*

Okies. For the next hour I let her have it, every single fear, worry, judgment, resentment, anger, you name it, she heard it, from my frustration with Quaid and Liam to the disgusting smarminess of the Dumont brothers to the creepy Darin and his stupid Star Club.

I might have been worried at first this would be too much for Sashenka, but the longer I went on, the more she nodded and murmured her sympathy and relaxed until I understood Sass was right. This was exactly what she needed.

To see you're human, he sent. *Or, mostly.*

Smart ass cat.

After I was done, we sat there in quiet for a bit while Sashenka reached out and took my hand, squeezing it gently. "I had no idea it was so hard for you."

I laughed then, feeling lighter and actually a little ashamed of myself, the way I'd been acting and thinking. "We all have our crap," I said. "Right?"

She flushed, dark skin rosy. "Yes," she said. Sighed. "I could just strangle Tallah sometimes."

We laughed together. This was more like it. Sashenka's smile stayed in place, a real smile, nothing fake about it, as she let go of my hand.

"A few of us are going out later," she said. "If you'd like to come?"

I hesitated immediately. I didn't want to ruin things for her and her friends. She might be understanding, but if what she said was true, would I make the others uncomfortable? The idea anyone was afraid of me almost made me giggle.

You won't know if you don't try. Sassafras leaped down from Sashenka's lap and waddled his fat cat body over to my bed where he hopped up and curled into a fluffy ball on my pillow.

I took the hint.

It was my first visit to the campus café and I had to admit I felt pretty nervous, even with Sashenka beside me and Charlotte guarding my back. The place was packed with other students, mostly freshmen from the excited looks on their faces. I almost backed out when the stares and whispers started all over again, but by then a small group of girls were waving and smiling at us and Sashenka had a firm grip on my hand, pulling me toward them, Charlotte standing off to one side and doing her best to look like a statue.

"Syd," my roommate gushed, "these are the girls. Girls, meet Sydlynn Hayle."

They stared a little, but were still smiling. The one on the right of the table with the curly dark hair and the palest skin I'd ever seen, offered her hand.

"Josie Ambrose," she said. "Hensley family. Nice to meet you."

That broke the ice. All at once I was introduced to Nicci

Mortimer (dirty blonde hair and a hand full of freckles on her cheeks), Donalda Pierce (tall and skinny, all elbows and knees though her long face was pretty because of her wide gray eyes) and Tippy Meeks (luscious red hair and curves I envied).

They pulled up an extra chair for me and proceeded to chatter on like I'd been their best friend forever. It was a little freaky, but pretty awesome at the same time. Though I admit after about a half hour of giggling over the latest movie star or peering at fashions I'd never be caught dead in on the screens of their iPhones, I was feeling a little overwhelmed.

"Don't look now but there's the Dumont brothers." Donalda actually snorted, long, thin nose twitching as if she'd smelled something awful that turned her stomach.

Tippy batted her long lashes, popping a large pink bubble from the gum she chewed with excessive aggression. "Too bad," she said. "All that jerk trapped in those delicious bods."

Sashenka giggled while I glared across the cafe at Jean Marc and Kristophe. Both waved at me, Kristophe tossing back his blonde hair to blow me a kiss before striking one of his model poses.

"Seriously," Nicci rolled her eyes, lips wrapped around

the straw of a soda as she looked heaven-ward. "No way, even if they suddenly turned nice. Gross."

Good to know I wasn't the only one who couldn't stand them. "They think they're all that."

Tippy leaned forward and grabbed my hand, showing off a bit more of her substantial cleavage than I would have liked. "Girl," she said, "I heard you've had some run-ins. Are they the kings of ew or what?"

"Totally." I found myself laughing despite the fact the Dumont brothers normally elicited anything but amusement from me. "Smarmy is the nicest word I can come up with."

The girls all giggled, and even Charlotte let out a soft laugh. Holy. Did I really make friends just like that? I had to thank Sashenka later. And Sass for making me deal with this.

I had to work on my trusting people skills.

Tippy flipped a wave at the boys. But when Kristophe winked at her and moved to join us Tippy's salute turned into a very rude gesture involving one very specific finger. I laughed out loud, eyes locked on the brothers as Kristophe scowled and turned away.

I know they would have left on their own. I felt the cold wave of disapproval heading their way, coming from most of the patrons of the cafe. It amazed me to realize no one really liked them.

How awesome was that?

I think that's why I cringed when Mia stormed into the cafe, blue eyes ablaze, and stomped her way up to the brothers. The ranting shrieks of fury following were enough to make everyone wince and turn away, pretending not to watch as the Dumont leader proceeded to make a fool of herself. The brothers slunk off half way through her screamfest and she followed them, still shouting orders at the top of her lungs which could be heard even through the door as it closed behind her.

The girls let out a collective sigh of relief. "I do not envy her that job," Nicci said, slurping up the last of her drink, shaking the ice on the bottom of her glass.

"Me either." Sashenka shuddered, turning to me. "She's a friend, isn't she?" They all looked at me with sympathy.

"Yes," I said, not ashamed to admit it. "I wish I could help her." The fun was gone out of me all of a sudden. It was clear Mia was out of control, had no hold over her coven at all if she was forced to perform such obvious displays in front of everyone.

I reached out to her, wanting to assist if I could. But the moment my mind touched hers, she slapped me away.

Mind your own business, Hayle. She slammed her shields against mine, hers flickering and violent as she struggled to control them. I'd forgotten how little she knew, how new she was to being a witch, much less a coven leader. Her power had been cut off her entire life, and only unsealed the night the Wild Hunt showed up at my house to destroy us all. She might have had some training with the best out there, namely my ex-Enforcer grandmother, but Mia was still only a newbie.

Thrown to the wolves. Or those who held wolves as slaves. Even worse.

Mia. I kept my tone calm though I wanted to beg her to listen. *If you need anything—*

If you try to interfere with me again, I'll file an official complaint with the Council. Like I'd tried to interfere. But she had her back up, because of the boys, and who knew what else.

I pulled away and let her go, heart heavy for my friend, but knowing there was nothing I could do. And yet, if the Dumont coven imploded, wasn't that everyone's problem? I made a mental note to mention it to Mom despite being fairly certain she wouldn't do a thing about it.

Class the next day was a totally different experience. Now that I had Liam and Sashenka with me, no one stared, or at least didn't stare for long. And I was able to escape the front row and Blanche Rhodes's attention by arriving early enough and hiding in the back with my friends beside me.

I ducked when I found her gaze searching for me and almost laughed at the sad little frown on her face. Liam poked me with a grin when the coast was clear.

He'd met us for breakfast and instantly apologized the moment he sat down.

"I was wrong," he said, eyes begging me to forgive him, big hands holding one of mine. "I just hate seeing him hurt you."

"I'm sorry too," I said. "It's not your fault he's a jerk sometimes."

I quickly introduced him to Sashenka who sat next to me, a small smile on her face. She seemed shy when he shook her hand, and I understood why. My Gatekeeper friend was pretty darned handsome and all that genuine sweetness oozing out of him could do a number on a girl.

I had a momentary jab of jealousy when she dimpled at his smile, but shoved it aside. Liam was my friend. If he and Sashenka decided to give things a go, I had no say in the matter.

Why then did I feel like I wanted to step between them and tell her he was mine?

The girls appeared pretty late, the three of us already up and leaving.

Tippy grinned and winked at Liam who blushed when she looked at him. "Syd, you didn't say anything about knowing someone tall, blonde and delicious."

Instead of feeling jealous, I laughed instead. I could tell by the way Liam pulled back from her, almost backing into me, as a matter of fact, he had absolutely no interest in the very forward red-head. I introduced him all around and though he was his normal kind and gentle self, I felt him sigh beside me as we walked to the library when we left them behind.

"We need to find you some guy friends," I laughed, punching him gently in the arm. "Before someone eats you up."

Liam blushed while Sashenka giggled behind her hands.

Despite the disappointment on Blanche's face when she finally spotted me, I resolutely held to my place in the back and dodged her questions as often as I could. She soon gave up on me and focused instead on her baby-talk teaching method which had me and my friends laughing and passing notes.

All of a sudden school was fun, more than fun. I even found a few of the students smiling at me, offering little waves as class let out, the same ones who stared and whispered the day before. I guess I was proving to them I wasn't so scary after all. Knowing it was fear holding them back, I smiled back, taking a page from Liam's book, doing my best to radiate friendliness and harmlessness.

Surprise, surprise, it seemed to be working. Even the Dumont brothers avoided me, slinking away after the door opened, and I wondered if Mia managed to pull the two of them under control after all. Who was I to know? Maybe yelling at them and humiliating them publicly was the only language they understood.

Second class found Liam and Sashenka going off together, but I had Tippy and Nicci to keep me company. Now that they knew who I was, and with Easton's permission, we worked together as a trio on our lab projects. Their back and forth, dry and sarcastic on one side and wickedly snarky on the other kept me giggling through the entire class.

I felt kind of bad for Charlotte as I left to go for lunch. I was so wrapped up in my new happiness I'd almost forgotten all about her. She was my friend, too, after all. When the girls passed her on the way out, I purposely hooked my arm through the weregirl's and pulled her alone beside me.

She tried to protest, but I shook my head. "This is what life is supposed to be like," I said. "For both of us." She was, after all, around the same age as me. Whoever made her who she was, taught her other people were more important than her… well. I knew who was to blame for her upbringing.

I lost Tippy and Nicci in the crowd, so intent on looking for them or my roommate and Liam as I crossed the Yard I stopped in my tracks when I locked eyes on Quaid. Not because it was him, but because he wasn't alone.

Not even remotely alone. He stood in the middle of a large group of, well, large guys and very capable looking girls, all who carried themselves like he did. Like they knew how to handle themselves. I started moving again, after spotting one of the girls, her long honey-blonde hair swinging forward as she leaned into Quaid with her big boobs and said something making him laugh.

Now I let my jealousy out. Who was that artificial cow

and what was she doing touching my boyfriend? I only peripherally noticed how other students seemed to avoid the group, going out of their way to keep clear. Maybe I didn't have the sense my mother gave me, because I stormed right into the middle of them and face-to-face with the guy who was supposed to be in love with me.

All laughter halted as I crossed my arms over my chest, unable to straighten the scowl from my lips. Even though most of the group towered over me, they all bowed their heads, murmuring, "coven leader," with great respect. I didn't want to be affected by their obviously deferential attention, but it was hard to stay mad with almost a dozen Enforcer trainees treating me like I was special.

Yeah, I was vain. So sue me.

The blonde girl, almost as tall as Quaid, was just as respectful so my jealousy took a hike. They had to be just friends. Especially when they all turned without having to be asked and moved off a short distance, far enough they wouldn't overhear our conversation, but close enough I knew they waited for him.

Well, wasn't that special?

With them gone, my anger came back. "Hi," I snapped. "Nice to see you."

Quaid nodded, head dropping. "I'm sorry," he said, very

softly in his voice like dark chocolate and velvet and I, naturally, forgave him right away.

Mostly.

My arms dropped, shoulders slumping a little. "I missed you," I said. "It's been a long summer without you. I wanted the first time I saw you again to be…"

"Special." He reached out, pulled me against his chest. This hug was much more what I was looking for, his full body welcoming me, chest warm and inviting, breath in my ear as he bent and pressed his lips to my skin. "I missed you so much, Syd."

"Looks like it." I jerked free of him, glancing at the group who pretended not to watch.

Quaid glanced their way too, sighed. "I know, I'm sorry. I'll introduce you to everyone, I promise." A happy light glowed in his dark eyes, picking up flecks of amber. "Syd, I had the most amazing time. Made fabulous friends. I feel like a real person for the first time… ever."

Which meant I didn't do it for him anymore? I held back my petulance. Quaid had the right to happiness, even more than I did. He'd been through so much in his life, being a power source for the people who raised him, having his real parents murdered by those same people. Finding out he was a Dumont and using his family ties to track down

Batsheva and Dominic Moromond. He'd spent his whole life on the outside. Who was I to judge him if he'd finally found a way in?

"That's great, Quaid." I really tried to mean it and from the smile on his face I did okay. There was a time when he wouldn't have bought it, would have seen past me and my crap. Not anymore, I guess.

"Just be nice to Liam, okay?" I sighed and let everything go. "He's my friend, Quaid."

His jaw tightened, but he nodded. "I know."

Okay, so I wasn't going to call him out either. Maybe we'd both changed.

"A movie tonight then?" I reached for his hand, let my demon magic out. She hummed happily, winding around his power, but he pulled back, making a sad face.

"I can't tonight." He glanced at his friends again. "I promised them. But tomorrow night? We can go for dinner first."

It was hard to accept they were more important. Because that's what he was telling me. He knew I'd want to be with him, but he made plans with them anyway. I looked over, found the blonde with the rack watching us. Her eyes were locked on Quaid and again a knife of anger drove through me.

"Well, have fun with your new girlfriend." I didn't mean it to come out, but I couldn't help it. Quaid grabbed my arm as I tried to turn away. I just wanted to escape him, leave him and his jerkish ways behind. When would I learn Quaid was really no good for me?

Until he pulled me tight again and kissed me, hot breath trickling down into my lungs as my lips parted without my permission and let him in.

"Syd," he said. "I love you. Don't ever forget that."

Hard to forget from this perspective. "I love you too." My throat tightened, tears threatening. But no way was I crying in front of him. I had to change the subject, keep him with me.

Why did I want to leave him again?

"Did you know Blood is here?" I stumbled over my words, desperate for some conversation suddenly to pin him to me. "His real name is Rupert. He and Simon are involved in some private club with a witch. I'm worried about them."

Quaid's frown was quick and dark as he let me go. "I thought we were talking about us?"

Crap. "We were." Damn it, what was wrong with me? "I just…"

Quaid shook his head, suddenly closing off, the connection between us going dim. "You know what, Syd? Just because bad stuff has found you in the past doesn't mean it's always around. Have fun, for once and stop looking for trouble."

He might as well have slapped me in the face. I was not imagining things nor was I asking for trouble thank you very much. Before I could shoot anything off at him in retaliation, he bent and kissed me quickly, awkwardly.

"I'll see you later, Syd." Quaid left, rejoined his friends, walked away without looking back.

I turned and left myself, doing everything I could to keep my fury and my tears on the inside.

Lunch was quiet, though Liam and Sashenka both tried several times to pull me out of my funk. I didn't really want to dump all over them over our sandwiches, not to mention if I did open up I'd end up sobbing my stupid face off, so instead I just shrugged off their concern and sat in my own little dark cloud of misery until next class.

This one I had with Sashenka, but it was easy enough to not talk while we focused on the work and the soothing sound of Isodore's voice, though the more I listened, the more I thought of Martin and Louisa and the worse my need to cry my heart out became.

I was really looking forward to Maryanne's class, for a chance to laugh again, to absorb some of her snarky fun, but it turned out to be canceled, a sign on the closed door saying she was sick. I waited a little while, just in case this was another of Albert Dumont's tricks, but when she didn't show, I instead retreated to the main library while Sashenka and the girls went off in search of a cup of coffee. I just needed to be alone.

I felt around for the hidden section housing the magical books, but only half-heartedly. Really if I found them, I'd only scope out a place to slide into the stacks and hide. As I was turning yet another corner, entering yet another huge room filled with tables and wide-backed chairs, I spotted Simon and Rupe hovering together with their heads together, whispering.

While I wanted to be alone, I also had to know what was up with them and took finding them as an opportunity to shake the depression weighing on me, if only for a little while. Funny how a mystery, the possibility of a problem, could suck me out of the dark and back into the real world.

Quaid's nasty remark hovered in the back of my mind as I walked over, refusing to believe what he'd said. I wasn't looking for trouble. I was trying to cut it off at the pass.

The moment I sat, my two friends looked up and immediately fell silent. In fact, both then lowered their heads over their books and refused to meet my eyes.

"Hey, guys." I didn't even pretend to pull out a book of my own. "How are you?"

Simon mumbled something I couldn't make out while Rupe's shoulders raised and lowered once. Okay then.

I was about to prod them further when I felt a familiar tingle of magic and looked up to find Charlotte hovering over me even as Darin and his two minions came to a halt beside Simon.

Despite what I'd done to his shields the last time we met, Darin still smiled at me like I'd be good to eat. He hadn't lost his arrogance with his personal wards. I prodded them and, to my shock, found them stronger than ever.

How did that happen? There was no way he'd be able to build himself up again so quickly. At least, not without help.

"Well, if it isn't Sydlynn Hayle." Darin leaned forward, face-to-face with me across the table. "How are you, little witch?"

His friends tittered a laugh, but Simon and Rupe remained silent.

"Better than you, I think." I sat back with my own smile. No way was this ass pushing me around. "At least I didn't have to have Mommy and Daddy rebuild my shields."

It had to be the explanation and, from the twitch of his lips, the unhappiness flashing through his eyes, I'd hit the bull's eye.

"You do know attacking another witch is a crime." His eyes went dark, angry, even as I continued to grin at him. Crime? Yeah, right. Nice threat, moron. "But I'm prepared to let it go."

"Oh really?" I studied the fingernails on my right hand, knowing he'd never report it, not when I could counter with his very forward greeting when we first met. Yeah, I might get a reprimand, but so would he.

Holy, my cuticles were a mess. I really had to stop biting them.

"Stay away from my initiates." Darin straightened, one hand falling on each of my friend's shoulders.

Something dark flashed on his wrist. "Nice tattoo," I said. "Not obvious or anything. Idiot."

When he turned his hand I caught another glimpse. The pentagram couldn't have been more plain.

Darin just grinned. "Maybe if you're good, we'll welcome you into the Star Club. Oh, wait." He laughed without humor. "You're a *girl*. Sorry, Syd. No girls allowed."

"What's the matter, Darin?" I leaned forward, letting my demon out into my eyes. The boys were still looking down so I had no fear they'd see. "Afraid just such a girl will kick your ass again?" I shouldn't have been talking so openly about our power in front of Rupe and Simon, but I couldn't help myself.

He snarled at me. "Watch your step, Syd." Darin backed up and my two friends rose immediately, arms full of books, still not looking at me. "Next time I'll report you."

I wasn't the only one speaking out of turn in front of normals. Oddly, neither of my friends seemed even remotely interested in the conversation. Which made me even more anxious.

What had Darin told them?

"You might want to think about that," I said. "Considering who the members of your club really are. And who my two friends happen to be." I knew he understood my meaning—he was a witch and Simon and Rupe were normals. What was he up to?

"Just mind your own business." I was surprised when Simon spoke up, more so because I'd heard those words from another friend not so long ago. "Darin's been my friend since I got here last year. He cares about me."

Sure he did. That nasty smile he gave me told me just how much Darin cared about Simon.

"Stay out of it, Syd." Rupe's deep voice had a petulant edge to it, something I'd never heard from him before. "We want to be in the Star Club."

Not much I could say to that.

Darin didn't comment further, just grinned at me like it was funny and swept off with his two minions and my friends in tow.

No trouble here, right?

Yeah. Right.

I sighed deeply, hearing Charlotte echo me. "Now I'm even more convinced something is going on."

She nodded, eyes locked on their retreating backs. "As am I."

I stood up, turned. Froze. Gaze locked on a girl walking into the stacks. I only caught a quick glimpse, just a flash of the side of her face, but I was sure. Positive. Without a shadow of a doubt.

Ameline.

Again.

I rushed after her without a word of warning to Charlotte, heart pounding as I pushed through a small knot of students and into the aisle. I practically ran all the way to the end, turned the corner.

Nothing. No one. Empty.

Charlotte grasped my arm, turned me to face her, her own expression unreadable.

"What is it." Not a question.

"Not what," I said. "Who. I saw her again."

I didn't have to tell Charlotte who I meant. She turned her head, lifted it, sniffed deeply. Met my eyes.

"I don't smell anything," she said.

Anger poured through my veins. "I bet it's just Darin

messing with me." He'd regret it if I caught him at it. And why was I so worried about the guys? They chose that smarmy jerk over me. Fine. They could have their boys only club with their loser of a leader.

I had better things to do.

18

By the time my day was over, I was in a better mood. Last class with Liam ended with him happily accepting my invitation to watch a movie later. Part of me felt guilty for making him my second choice again, but since we were just friends I didn't really let it get to me.

He arrived with a box of microwave popcorn and a giant chocolate bar, all for me. It was hard not to love him for stuff like that.

We curled up in the empty commons in front of the TV on the puffy leather couch with a shared blanket over our knees, laughed, stuffed ourselves on popcorn and just had fun. Charlotte had agreed to stay in her room and just leave us alone for a while and I was very grateful. I forgot how much I loved spending time with Liam, how easy our friendship had become and was very, very thankful to have him in my life.

Now, if only I could get Quaid out of my head.

Sashenka disturbed us briefly, hanging over the edge of the couch with a big smile on her face.

"Party later," she said. "At one of the Houses for the upperclassmen. You guys want to come?"

We both shook our heads immediately. Was I really so much of a homebody? But the warmth and earthiness of Liam's magic was fused to mine where his leg pressed against my thigh. Leaving the comfort of our little nest seemed ridiculous.

She left quickly and we went back to our movie.

Or tried to. When I turned back, I found Liam watching me with a smile on his face.

"What?" I tossed some popcorn at him, laughing.

"I'd rather be here with you, too," he said. And kissed me.

Everything went away. Everything. Shaylee's Sidhe magic surged forward, wrapping around us like a cloak, pulling Liam closer, bonding our power together. His firm lips tasted of salt and butter and chocolate, kiss loving and as sweet as he was. His warm breath tickled the inside of my mouth, one hand settling on my shoulder, pulling me gently toward him, tip of his nose hot against my cheek. I leaned into it, fingers tracing over the side of his face, feeling the smooth, soft skin, so different from the roughness of Quaid's—

I jerked away the moment Liam did. We stared at each

other for a long time while emotions I couldn't begin to sort out raged through my body. Cold and suddenly hot, cold again in a flash, I hugged myself as I felt horror slide over my face.

"Syd." Liam cleared his throat, hand reaching for me only to drop again. "Syd, I'm sorry. It... I never meant..."

Before I could say or do anything, he rose to his feet, the blanket falling from his lap. Shoulders slumped, head down, Liam practically ran from the commons and disappeared through the door.

Oh. My. Swearword. What was that? Did we really...? And I.

Oh. My. Swearword.

I. Liked. It.

I was on my feet, pacing in front of the couch, feet tangling in the blanket now sprawled on the floor, spilled bowl of popcorn spread over the cushions. I kissed Liam. Liam kissed me. And we both liked it.

What the hell?

I shook my head. Okay, I had to admit, I'd always been attracted to Liam. Right from day one when I helped him find his first class. But that was just the Sidhe power talking. Wasn't it?

Wasn't it?

A secret, private, quiet part of my heart reminded me of something I'd admitted long ago. If Quaid wasn't around, I could easily have fallen in love with Liam.

Was I in love with him anyway?

No. I loved Quaid. Loved him with all of my heart. Gave him my heart, in fact. Which he stomped on and trampled and cast aside—

Damn it, Syd. Get a freaking grip.

I couldn't think, couldn't just pace there alone with the memory of my magic and Liam's all wrapped up together, with the taste of him still on my mouth. I wiped carefully at my lips with the sleeve of my shirt before running from the room.

Back to my dorm and Sashenka who was just leaving.

The party. Right.

"Change your mind?" Her smile faded a little. I must have looked so panicked. I know I felt panicked.

"Yes," I said, grabbing a sweater. "Party. Perfect." I had to get this out of my head, had to forget what I'd done before I lost my mind. "Let's go."

Why are parties all the same? Indoor, outdoor, normals, witches—didn't seem to matter. Put a bunch of kids together without supervision and access to alcohol and kablooie, instant mess.

I was beginning to accept the fact I was just a prude and there was nothing I could do about it. Or wanted to for that matter. Especially when I was in the kind of headspace where everything sucked.

Oh, I tried to fit in with the upperclassmen, even accepted a glass of cold beer just so they'd stop offering. It quickly warmed, but that was okay because I had no intention of sampling the stuff. A few sniffs told me the bouquet hadn't improved since my first encounter with it, the night Suzanne, the cheer squad leader, had summoned up the spirit of Cesard and turned that particular party into a mass exodus of screaming teenagers.

Still, it was better being here at the party, surrounded by a crowd of drunk people, often shoved or bumped into or toes trodden on than being back in my dorm, stewing over the fact Liam kissed me.

Yes, he kissed me. Not the other way around. I'd decided by the time the door to the House opened and Sashenka and I walked in to the loud and smoky place I was simply an innocent bystander in the whole kissing incident and the moment I saw him again I'd slap him for it.

Yeah, Syd. Okay. Whatever.

I finally set aside my full glass of pale yellow disgustingness, almost clinging to Sashenka who had the good taste to be drinking a soda herself. At least I thought it was soda. If she chose to add something to it, that was up to her. But witches were notorious for not being able to hold their liquor and since Uncle Frank had as yet to take me out into the middle of nowhere like he promised and get me drunk so I couldn't hurt anyone, just to see what happened, I wasn't risking it.

It didn't take me long to realize this was my worst choice of distractions. The music was so loud I could barely think, driving into my skull almost like a physical attack, making me feel agitated and angry. Charlotte pressed so close to my back at times I wanted to spin on her and snarl. But it wasn't her fault. She was here to protect me, just doing her job.

I had just turned to tell her we were leaving when I spotted the Dumont brothers oozing toward me. But instead of stopping to torment me as I expected they would, Jean Marc made oogle eyes at Tippy while Kristophe reached out and touched Sashenka's cheek.

My magic flared, demon roaring for me to act and I almost did. Almost. But these girls weren't frail and fragile flowers, weren't easily thralled normals like the damaged Page or the equally screwed-up Alison. They were witches, from powerful families.

Tippy leaned toward Jean Marc, her ruby lips moving. She laughed when he jerked back from her, scowling. Whatever she said to him set her friends off. Nicci giggled beside her while Donalda howled so loud I heard her over the music.

Sashenka merely smiled at Kristophe before tipping her full glass down the front of his pants.

Okay, maybe parties weren't so bad after all.

I might actually have even had fun at that point, just basking in the glow of the Dumont brother's humiliation, if I hadn't looked up and caught sight of Quaid across the room. With his friends.

And the honey-blonde hanging from his arm, her lips against his ear.

Fireworks went off in my head, practically tearing me

apart. His eyes caught mine and widened just as I spun and forced my way through the crowd, pushing against Charlotte who eased aside and let me go. Fury raged through my veins, burning me from the inside out. So this is why he couldn't be with me? Some party? And her? More fun than me, okay, I got it. Message received, loud and clear.

Liam's face flickered in my mind, but I dodged it. Not my fault. And that damned kiss never would have happened if my so-called boyfriend hadn't ditched me to party with his friends.

I felt the connection between Quaid and I tighten, the touch of his mind on mine, but I was so not even going there with him tonight. So. Not. He could simmer in his guilt or whatever he was feeling and leave me the hell alone.

I slammed the connection shut, delivering a blow to his magic I know made him stagger. Screw him.

Just screw him.

Charlotte kept silent when I reached for the veil and grasped her hand. No way was I walking back to my dorm. Not in the state I was in. Not even thinking about the consequences, I parted reality, the rubbery membrane between Demonicon and my plane welcoming me as I slid inside it and rode it, Charlotte beside me, back to the Yard.

We stepped out only a heartbeat later and I longed to go back inside it, to run for home, to Wilding Springs and my own bed, to Gram and the coven and the Wild Hunt sleeping in my back yard.

But no way was I running. Not from some asshole guy who'd broken my heart more times than I could remember all for his own stupid agenda. No. Freaking. Way.

SYDLYNN THADDEA HAYLE. Mom's angry connection was so loud I had to grit my teeth. *Do not EVER do that again.*

I'm a demon, I shot back at her. No way was she bossing me around in that tone. *I'll ride the veil any time I feel like it.*

Oh boy. Was she mad. Like, not normal Mom mad, but wild animal ready to tear something apart with her teeth and claws mad.

Never. Again. Her boiling touch vanished, leaving me fuming even more. How dare she reprimand me like that? She'd used an open channel, too. Any witch in five miles would have heard her.

So public humiliation was her new game, was it?

We'd see about that.

"Are you done broadcasting or do you plan to burn the place down?"

I jerked to a halt, looked up, startled to see Sassafras

perched on the lowest branch of a nearby tree. The sight of him made my heart clench.

Fury turned to absolute crushing grief. No crying. No.

"Don't tempt me." There, that was better. Finding my anger always kept me level.

"Hmm." Sassy hopped down, using magic as he floated softly to the ground. As always, when he used his magic, the flicker of the boy he used to be appeared briefly in a halo around him. "I think your mother would not approve."

"In case you missed it," I said with sharp sarcasm, "she doesn't." I clenched my jaw against the need to shoot back at her, using him as my sounding board instead. "Mom can bite me." My whole body shook, the occasional firecracker still going off in my head as my skin tingled with the need to hurt something. Someone.

"Syd." Sassy came to stand at my feet, stretching himself upward, claws hooking in my jeans. "Up."

I hesitated, not ready to have my fury diffused. But I couldn't resist his amber eyes, the way his ears flattened sideways, whiskers drooping. I finally scooped him into my arms and let him head-butt me gently.

"Are you all right?" His tone was soft, the barest purr emerging. "I felt your hurt long before your mother blew a gasket."

No. Freaking. Crying.

"Fine." I swallowed hard. "It's nothing."

"It's not nothing." He glanced at Charlotte who had the sense to keep her mouth shut. "Quaid?"

Now I was trembling for another reason. "I don't want to talk about it."

Sassy sighed. "This is the hardest part of my job, you know that?" One paw gently touched my cheek. "The heart stuff."

I could only imagine. Generations of Hayle witches had come and gone for him. "I'm not the only one, huh?"

"Not by a long shot." His purr rose in volume, but I blocked the demon magic he tried to use to influence me.

"I'll be okay," I said, setting him down. "I promise." I did feel better, but didn't want to, not yet. Stupid, maybe. Still. "I just need to figure this out on my own."

Sassy's tail thrashed once. "As you wish."

Charlotte hissed softly before I could turn to walk up the steps to my dorm. "Is that who I think it is?"

Yup, sure was. Rupe and Simon, sneaking off again.

"None of my business," I said even as I felt drawn to follow them.

"What isn't?" Sassafras's golden gaze watched them too. "What's going on?"

I filled him in quickly as the pair disappeared across the Yard.

"I don't like the sound of that," Sassy said. "Let's follow. I want to get a look at where they are going."

I lifted him into my arms again, grasped Charlotte's hand and went back into the veil. Mom's orders or not, no way was I running to chase the boys, not when I had other means of travel at my disposal. For an instant, while we rode the veil, Sassafras's body weight seemed to increase almost to the point I couldn't hold him. Enough of who he had been survived, it seemed, tied to his magic, though I knew he would never be a demon again.

We stepped out of the veil in the same patch of darkness we hid in the night before just in time to see Rupe and Simon climb the stairs to the door. I clenched up inside, prepped for another screaming lecture from Mom, but none came. Maybe she'd relented? I didn't have time to wonder or care. This time when my friends knocked, Darin greeted them personally and gestured for them to enter. Sassafras's low growl made the hair on the back of my neck and arms stand up.

"Something's not right here," he whispered. "Do you feel those wards?"

I flushed a little, realizing I'd not considered checking

them out previously. I quickly corrected my mistake, reaching out to feel along the edges of the building.

Witch wards, certainly. They felt like Darin, only stronger. His father? But those weren't the only ones guarding the house.

White power sizzled along the edges, and the contained virus around my neck stirred at its touch.

"No way," I said. "How can that be?"

"I don't know," Sassafras said, tone grim, "but we need to tell your mother Darin's family is connected to a clan of vampires."

I couldn't make myself move. "There's nothing wrong with that," I said at last. "We're associated with a clan. Hell, my uncle is one of them."

Sassy just glared at the house. "There's a treaty here, remember? No vampires allowed. And yes, it's only meant to protect the Yard, but all of the clans are to stay away from this entire school."

Charlotte's nostrils flared as she snuffled the air. "I admit, I've been feeling uneasy," she finally said, "but there's been nothing concrete. I haven't felt any vampires, not blatantly. Perhaps the wards are old, left over from a former association."

It was pretty clear from their strength how fresh the shields were, so she was wrong.

"We have to inform Miriam." Sassy finally turned away from his observation, meeting my eyes with his, the deep glow of his power shining in the darkness.

I wasn't about to argue with him because I agreed one

hundred percent. A quick slip through the veil put us back in the Yard. Surprisingly, there was no reaction from my mother. Maybe she was accepting she couldn't box me in with her stupid rules. Either that or she'd had an aneurysm from my disobedience. Still, she'd left it wide open, so it was her own fault. By allowing my power to pass through the wards surrounding the school, she'd basically told the old magic protecting Harvard riding the veil was A-okay.

The elevator dinged and we were off it within moments of leaving the boys behind at the club house. Charlotte snarled at the entry to the sitting room and slammed to a halt.

"Still can't enter," she said.

Nice. "Sorry," I said. "I'll deal with it, I promise."

She shrugged but not because she wanted me to forget it. "Just tell her what you need to."

I hated leaving her behind like a servant but had little choice in the matter. Sassafras leaped down from my arms and bounded off toward the dining room so I followed him though I caught sight of him sliding between Maurice's legs even as the unhappy little man glared at me from behind his glasses and blocked my way with his pudgy body and one upraised hand.

"Can I help you?" He sniffed the air as if I'd brought some horrible odor with me. "Miss Hayle?"

"I need to see Mom." I was still furious with her, but even I knew something was up and had to take the higher road in order to have something done about it. But Maurice blocking me from reaching her? Yeah, that wasn't going to happen.

I tried to push past him but his power was tied to the shields on the house. He might have been no match for me alone, but with the magic of the entire Council behind him I was out of luck.

"The Council Leader is in meetings at the moment and cannot be disturbed." He gave me a look telling me there was no way I was as important as a Council meeting and that he would do everything in his power to keep me from reaching my mother.

We'd see how that worked out for him.

Mom. I grasped for her mind even as I slid into the veil and used it to slip past Maurice. Would it piss her off further? Likely. Only a flicker of movement, but it was enough to stir the shields in the building. Mom must have been trying to differentiate between who I was and what I could do, but clearly wasn't getting it quite right. It felt like she'd gone too far the other way, choosing the safety of the school over mine.

And what exactly did that say about her?

Before the wards could boot my ass out of the building, Mom swept into the sitting room with a very angry look on her face. Sassafras stood at her side, eyes glowing, a low snarl coming from him. For a brief moment I thought perhaps it was her secretary she was angry with. How dare he keep me from my mother? Until her snapping blue eyes settled on me and the same old, same old judgments came pouring out of her, fed by her new fury at my lack of obedience.

"Sydlynn," Mom snapped like I was ten and broke her favorite vase. "What is the meaning of all this?"

One glance at Sassafras told me he hadn't the chance to fill her in, or cool her off after my little veil riding argument. I skimmed over that, telling her everything I'd learned about Darin and the Star Club, how my two friends were involved as quickly as I could, trying to rein in my temper even as my demon cat added his own concerns to mine.

When we were done, Mom's anger had dimmed, though she still looked irritated. The secretary huffed beside me as he pushed past me and joined Mom, almost like they were closing ranks. Well, I had my own ranks, thank you. So what if he was a fluffy ball of silver fur?

"I understand your concern for your friends," Mom said. "And the fact there are vampires in the vicinity. But," she held up one index finger, the most annoying gesture I'd ever seen her make, "since the wards you speak of and the club house itself are off Yard property, they aren't breaking any laws."

"Miriam," Sassafras started but Mom cut him off.

"It's troublesome," she said. "Not only the vampire presence, but the fact witches are luring normals into their clubs. Still, it's possible there aren't dark motives involved and they are simply seeking to expand their membership. That isn't illegal either, as long as they don't reveal who they are." It was my turn to try to talk, but Mom pushed on. "I'll look into it. Thank you for bringing this to my attention." Mom's eyes fixed on me. "Now, why don't you go back to your dorm room and focus on school and having fun? This is a very important year for you, sweetheart, a time when you make allies and friends among other witches you would never normally have time to meet. And you've been through enough trouble already. No more riding the veil, no more magical displays. Just leave this to me."

Oh no she did *not* just practically repeat what Quaid said to me. I was not looking for trouble.

Damn it. She was just humoring me.

Mom turned and left, Maurice already moving toward me, herding me out. I didn't resist. Why bother? Not like Mom was willing to listen to me anyway.

Besides, I'd done what I could, Sassy and I both had. If this turned into a giant mess, let Mom clean it up. She couldn't say I didn't tell her so.

We were back on the elevator, Charlotte's anger matching mine, when Sassafras kyboshed the thoughts going through my head.

"We can't break the wards on another witch's domain and you know it." He growled softly. "Not without cause." When he sighed, his tail thrashed in time with the sound. "I don't know what's gotten into your mother, but she's so tied to the big picture she's started to ignore the details."

"Oh, so that's what you call it." I was a detail. Two normals and maybe more being sucked into who knew what by a witch I didn't trust was a detail.

Lovely.

"I'll watch the place myself," Sass said as we left the building and headed for my dorm. "I don't trust this one bit."

That at least made me feel better, though after he scampered off into the darkness I missed him immediately.

21

Charlotte kept her distance as I started walking. Not toward my dorm, not yet. I couldn't sleep yet. Instead I began a slow circle of the Yard, head down, eyes locked on the path, but mind far away as I struggled with my emotions. Now that Sassafras was on the job with the boys, all of the pain and confusion came rushing back.

We had only gone half way around the circle, tall trees drenching the Yard in deep shadows, when Charlotte's soft hiss pulled me to a halt. I looked up and caught sight of Quaid outside what had to have been his dorm.

With her. The honey-blonde pressed against his arm, a low laugh reaching me through the dark and quiet. He laughed in return, head bent toward her. An intimate moment, one reminding me of the same connection he and I shared.

I wanted to be angry, to be jealous. But as I stood there in the night and forced myself to gulp cool air while I watched the guy I loved with another girl, my heart, already in trouble when it came to Quaid, shrank and cracked in half.

Charlotte's gentle hand on my arm turned me around, forcing me to look away. "He's not worthy," she growled.

I shrugged and glanced their way again. They hadn't kissed or anything, at least not that I'd seen. Was I overreacting? Looking for trouble, just like he said?

I let Charlotte lead me home, slipped into my room, grateful Sashenka was still out. But I didn't sleep, couldn't. Tried a few times to lie down only to toss and turn and leap up again while my mind and what was left of my heart tortured me over Quaid. Was she still with him? Did he love me anymore or had things really changed? I hadn't felt it from him. The connection between us was still there. Surely if he didn't love me, if he wanted to be with her, he'd have severed our magical touch.

Wouldn't he?

I couldn't stand it anymore. I had to see him, talk to him. And not just using magic. I needed to be able to touch him, to look in his eyes when I asked him the hard questions. The ones I didn't want to ask.

But I also couldn't have Charlotte hovering and watching, either. A brief shot of guilt was all I allowed myself as I fetched my sweater and sent out a very subtle, very gentle touch of magic across the hall.

Charlotte wasn't sleeping, not really. Her mind was more in some kind of meditation mode. Did she ever sleep? All it took was a very soft push and she was out like a light.

I still snuck as quietly as I could past her door, just in case, not breathing a sigh of relief until I was out the door of the Hall and in the Yard. Free, a new kind of dread took me over. Was I ready for what Quaid might tell me?

My feet dragged over the grass as I forced myself to cross to his dorm, wrapping myself in a bit of magic to make sure no one saw me. I felt like I was breaking some kind of law, or doing something wrong, but I had to know, had to see him.

No matter what the cost.

I was forced to wait in the shadows while two freshmen, normals from the look of them, passed through the main door before I reached out and felt around for Quaid. His power latched onto mine immediately, but it was clear from his touch he wasn't alone.

I bit back a sob, only to realize there were multiple people with him, not just her. It made things a little easier when his mind touched mine, gentle, tender.

Give me two seconds.

I felt him through the connection as he continued to hold onto me, banish his friends from his room. His power cradled me like I was something precious until he was alone again.

I didn't bother using the entry, but rode the veil right to his door. Mom could just suck it up. And when she didn't comment or even seem to notice, I forgot about her entirely. My entire body clenched as I stood there for the single heartbeat it took for Quaid to reach his door, turn the knob, wrench it open.

The moment his eyes met mine all of my questions were answered. The love in the deep chocolate of his gaze drew me to him just as much as his strong hands as he reached out with his power and his body to pull me into his arms and kiss me like he'd missed me as much as I missed him.

I'm so afraid. I clung to him, the fire of his lips on mine making me shaky. *I don't want to lose you.*

Syd, Syd. His mind was wide open, his heart, for the first time completely and I could see and feel, as clearly as if it were my own, just how much he loved me.

Tears welled, spilled over, ran down my cheeks. He kissed them away, holding me even tighter, rocking me slightly as we stood there at the threshold of his room while his love for me filled me up so much I could barely breathe.

Yes. This. This true love, this feeling, the way we were perfect together, how our magic linked and meshed and flowed like we were two parts of the same whole. He was kissing me again, his hands touching me in ways I'd always wanted them to. There had always been something in our way before, some crisis or disaster, but here, now, for the first time, it was just me and Quaid and our love.

He didn't resist when I pushed him back into his room and kicked the door shut behind us.

22

My whole body was warm, tingly. It felt odd yet amazing at the same time to wake to the touch of him pressed against me, skin soft and rough, stirring up all kinds of fabulousness. Light and heat touched my face, forcing my eyes to flicker open and blink into the morning sunlight. I stretched, sighing in happiness, everything about this particular morning absolutely perfect.

I'd been worried about us why? Hard to recall with the guy I loved snuggled up beside me, bare chest so delicious I wanted to eat him up, the pentagram tattoo I adored dark in the morning light. While I may have been running on total instinct last night, it was clear Quaid at least had some prior experience. And though a sad little part of me wished it had been our first time together, my happy body was quite pleased he'd known what he was doing.

Shiver.

Yes. Perfect. Everything had been perfect. Including the thrill of magic tying us together, magic that had nothing to do with the connection we already shared. Was there something to this destiny stuff after all? Were Quaid and I meant for one another, fated and did the zing of power mean we were finally bonded forever?

As much as that kind of magic would have bothered me any other time, for once I welcomed it. Quaid was mine, all mine, would be for as long as we both lived. It was hard not to secretly hear wedding bells and fantasize about what our kids would look like as I lay there next to him, letting our lives stretch out in front of me until we were crotchety old people, still desperately in love, hand in hand on our front porch while we snarked at the neighbor's kids.

Quaid's handsome face glowed as he smiled with half-lidded eyes from the pillow next to me. His dark hair hung over his cheek and I took a lazy moment to sweep it aside before leaning over to kiss him.

"Morning." His lips curved in a tasty line, begging for more. My demon shivered in anticipation, growling softly while I felt heat rise to the surface of my skin even as my world narrowed down to one single vision. Quaid.

I opened my mouth to answer and broke into giggles before covering my mouth with both hands as a race of nerves I was really here, right now, with him, the image of us as a happy old couple vanishing as I realized where I was and what we'd done. Contemplating a repeat performance of last night. This time I was without the emotional surge to push me through my butterflies. Why was I nervous? This was Quaid, the guy I loved and would do anything for.

Still. "Crap," I said, making an excuse for my laughter. "Morning breath."

Quaid grabbed me and pulled me close, so close I could focus on nothing but the hunger in his dark eyes.

Turns out morning breath and excited butterflies weren't really much of an issue.

I was going to be late for class, but somehow I didn't really care all that much. Quaid's shower was plenty big for the two of us, turned out, and he was more than willing to share. Share? Um, well, more like he couldn't stand to let me out of his arms for even a second.

And I was all for that.

Any fears or confusion I'd felt were long gone, my heart doing a happy tap dance every time he touched me, looked at me, came close to me. And that was a near constant. It was impossible to doubt how perfect we were together while he kissed the inside of my wrist after I finished tucking my wet hair into a messy bun at the nape of my neck, or when he pressed those amazing lips to the corner of my mouth, making my cheek tingle from the roughness of his scruff.

Delicious. Did I mention he was delicious? Yum.

Heart full and feeling his power with me as strong as ever, stronger even if that was possible, I contentedly strolled out of the building with him, hand-in-hand, into the gorgeous morning sunlight. Quaid pulled me close and kissed me, slow and long and lingering, until my knees threatened to give way and my heart was racing so fast I was sure I'd die from happiness.

"I love you." His dark eyes were so intent it was almost as if he doubted I believed him.

I gripped his handsome face between my hands and sent him everything I was feeling through my magic, including the naughty thoughts my demon was having as she purred in absolute delight.

"I know," I said. "Quaid, I love you too. You felt it?"

The magic binding us together, the very fate Mom always secretly smiled about. He nodded slowly. "And here I thought your mother was just trying to control us."

I snorted, kissed him again. "You and me, Quaid. Forever and always. We're meant to be."

He smiled then, kissed the tip of my nose. The light touch made me giggle.

"We're both late," he said, but his tone told me he cared about as much as I did.

"Yeah," I said. "Oh well."

I'm not sure how long we would have stood there, grinning at each other like idiots, if Quaid's Enforcer friends hadn't shown up. But I was in such a great mood, his love still wrapped around me, I didn't feel a flicker of resentment as he finally turned and left, hand holding mine to the last possible moment until his fingertips were all I had of him.

I hugged myself as he waved, walking backwards as he retreated, eyes locked on me. I wanted to jump up and down, squeal like a little girl, tell someone, anyone, how much I loved him. How yes, we were right for each other, he was the perfect guy for me. Bouncy and full of the most joy I'd ever felt, I drifted my way across the Yard to my own dorm to fetch my book bag.

And came face-to-face with a very, very angry Charlotte.

Oh, crap.

She handed me my bag, jaw so tight I was certain she'd shatter it, and refused to speak one word to me, even when I tried to apologize. I didn't let her attitude get me down. She'd just have to get used to the fact there would be times I needed my privacy.

Hopefully tonight, in fact. The memory of Quaid made

me blush and giggle to myself just as I sank into a seat in my first class. Sashenka raised an eyebrow but she was smiling.

"Where were you last night?" Her eyes flickered to Liam who sat on the other side of me.

Liam. Right. His hazel eyes met mine as I tried to dampen my enthusiasm.

"Out." I could have just said Mom's, but I didn't want to lie to her. And there was no way I was telling her I was with Quaid with Liam sitting right there. I was happy and loved Quaid, but after what happened the night before, I wasn't about to hurt my Sidhe friend by going on and on about my boyfriend.

But it did remind me we had to talk about what happened. Liam acted like nothing changed, but now that Quaid and I were on solid ground again, I needed to deal with my friend and his feelings.

It was hard not to let my mind wander to Quaid and I found myself doodling his name as if I were some pre-teen with a crush. Liam acted funny all day, sitting next to Sashenka instead of me, head down, not talking. My guilt began to grow, cutting through my happiness at last, added to the continuing cold shoulder Charlotte gave me until I finally felt like a criminal or something.

I finally headed back to my room after classes were over, begging off when Sashenka and the girls invited me to the cafeteria with them. Liam left without a word before I could chase him down. Selfishness won in the battle between hunting him down and making him talk to me and reaching for Quaid.

No surprise there.

The moment I sent my magic to Quaid I knew something was wrong.

Are you okay? He felt angry and frustrated.

I'm fine. His mental voice snapped. Then softened. *Sorry, rough day.*

Can I help? I let my demon reach for him, but he cut her off, tightening the connection between us until only a thin thread remained.

Thanks, but I can handle this myself.

Okay then. *Are you sure? I'm happy to—*

I don't need a coven leader to save me, thanks. Quaid's mental voice sighed as I gasped softly. He might as well have slapped me, it hurt so much. *Syd, I'm sorry, really. Just… give me a little space tonight. I'm not fit to be around. Okay?*

Okay. I knew I should just pull away, let him have the space he wanted, but my heart, still freshly full of love, needed reassurance since we'd just declared our undying devotion to each other, both in heart and body. The fate thing, right? *I love you.*

He paused. Paused. Only an instant, but that instant was a lifetime.

I love you, too. And then, he was gone.

And my fragile and wide-open heart wanted to die. Just whither and collapse and let go of everything, shatter and turn to dust so I didn't have to feel what I was feeling. Worry the magic connecting us, the destiny I was so sure of was a lie after all, some distortion of what might have been—choke—for him at least, just sex.

It took a long time for me to talk myself down. I pushed myself into the corner where my bed met the wall and hugged my knees to my chest, trying to hold myself together when I was sure I was about to fly apart. I'd never, ever been so vulnerable, not when my demon left me, not when my family was in danger, never. Not like this.

Never like this.

Syd. Sassafras's voice shook me out of the spinning wheel of thoughts holding me hostage. *I've been watching the house and there's no activity. I'm just going to head back to visit Meira then I'll join you.*

Okay. I kept my thought tight. The last thing I needed was a lecture from my demon cat. *Thanks.*

Maybe Quaid was right. I was looking for trouble because that was my life, all I knew. Both with him and with Darin's little club. My body started to relax, the panic holding me thrall easing as I let my head fall forward, forehead pressed to my knees. I was being silly. Quaid was allowed a bad day. Goodness knew I'd had enough of my own. I was being an idiot.

And yet, I couldn't let it go. Couldn't. I headed for my door, felt for Charlotte. She was in her room, stewing. I'd really pissed her off. But I needed time alone, really alone, to walk and think without her hanging off of me.

Who was I kidding? I was going to Quaid's and didn't want her around.

It was a little harder to put her to sleep this time, but I managed, guilt at my act much stronger than it had been. She was only doing her job, or what she thought was her duty. She'd been manipulated and used by the Dumonts her whole life and here I was doing the same thing to her. I swore to myself as I chose to sneak past her room rather than risk Mom's wrath by sliding into the veil, I'd sit down with her later and tell her everything.

She had to understand.

23

I made it all the way across the Yard and to Quaid's dorm only to reach for him and find out he wasn't even home. Which naturally made my mind spin in circles wondering where he'd gone and who he was with.

The image of the honey-blonde hanging off him, her oversized chest pressed to his arm made my skin tight with pent-up anxiety. I'd already accepted while it had been my first time, this wasn't Quaid's first romp under the sheets. The juvenile idea he'd had condoms in his room just for the two of us now seemed totally ridiculous, another lie I told myself. Was he with her now? No way was I sleeping, not with worst-case scenarios playing out in my head.

I know I should have gone back to my dorm and fetched Charlotte, but I couldn't bring myself to go back, just in case I ran into Sashenka and had to try to explain. And I was in no mood to fight with my bodywere either. Once she found out I'd knocked her out for the second time so I could sneak off, I'd suffer for it, I was sure.

Besides, I really needed to be alone to torture myself correctly. Wouldn't do to have a possible shoulder to cry on nearby, would it? Naw, better to simmer in my own pity party privately than ask for help or something.

Or reach for Quaid. That I refused to do. No way was I turning into the clingy girlfriend. Okay, clingier. Though I had to give myself kudos for not badgering him all summer at all aside from our weekly Skype chats and daily emails.

I was a good girlfriend, damn it, gave him lots of space. Too much?

Sigh. I just couldn't win.

Your sister is asleep. Sassy's mental voice broke my mental pacing even as I walked the Yard, keeping to the shadows. *I'm heading toward you now.*

A moment of guilt ran through me. Right. My sister. And then my mind went to Rupe and Simon. I had other things I could be thinking about right now. And other people I cared about who deserved some attention. Clearly Quaid didn't.

I'm tired. Sassafras's tone was a little sharp. *I hope you're keeping the pillow warm for... where are you?*

Oops.

Out. I tried for authoritative, to let him know I didn't care one way or the other what he thought of my little stroll even as I crossed out of the Yard and headed for Memorial Church.

Sassy ignored my tone. *Tell me you have Charlotte with you.*

How did he know I'd left her behind? Did he know about last night?

My cheeks flushed bright red at the thought my demon cat knew I'd stayed the night with Quaid.

Oh, get over yourself. Sassy's mental voice sniffed with arrogance only he could pull off. *I've been around more hormonal young witches than you, Sydlynn. But Charlotte is with you for a reason.*

I'm perfectly safe here. I stopped and looked up at the church, almost glowing white in the light of the full moon. The place kind of gave me the creeps.

That's not the point. He huffed in my head. *I'm coming to meet you. Don't move.*

Smart ass cat. Like he could do anything I couldn't. Wasn't I part witch, part demon, part Sidhe princess? I was fairly certain I could take care of myself, thanks.

Something flickered down the path, closer to the church, and I found myself gasping for a lost breath, hands pressed to my chest in fright as a row of young soldiers suddenly appeared out of thin air and marched past me. They didn't notice me, the echoes of the Northern Civil War troops only lasting a few steps before they faded out again, but the sight of them was enough to freak me out.

The chill air and absolute emptiness they left behind raised goosebumps on my arms and filled me with deep sadness. I'd find no resolution out here, in the dark, alone. Only an aching heart that refused to let go of Quaid and worried for Liam, growing fear and doubt bouncing between the two boys in my life and making my heart ache.

My emotions finally turned me around. Maybe Sass was right. This place was really old, the oldest campus on the continent. Who knew what lurked where? And though I was sure nothing here could harm me, I wasn't exactly a fan of getting the pants scared off of me either. Or of wallowing. It used to be my way, but I was getting pretty tired of the whole poor me thing.

I could feel Sassafras's approach as he bounded across the Yard toward me and finally stepped out of the darkness to meet him. The moment I did, I felt the vampire virus shudder against my skin. Not the light vibration I'd gone through before. This was a violent reaction, as if the entity inside was suddenly wide awake and fighting me again.

But that wasn't possible. It should be sound asleep. I looked down in horror at the bright glow of it almost burning through the fabric of my sweater as I layered more power over it. But it ignored me, bouncing and struggling against my controls.

No. Way. I'd poured so much power over it, the source of the virus should have slept for centuries. Unless… unless it sensed vampires. And not just nearby, and not just one or two. No, they had to be many and right on top of—

I barely had time to raise my personal shielding before the air around me shuddered and a dozen vampires shifted out of shadow to surround me.

24

My demon roared in fury, lashing out on her own while I fought the now screeching virus. Shaylee tapped the earth, driving blades of green fire up around me, forming a circle of protection even as my demon sent a sheet of pure amber power out toward the attacking vampires.

For an instant I worried they were friendly. Were we attacking Sebastian's clan by accident? But that fear was gone the moment one of the vampires lunged forward through the power barriers and struck me.

Wait a second. How…? I staggered backward, jerking the virus in its marble gem free and clutching it in my hand, the brightness of its glow streaming out from between my fingers like I attempted to contain a blazing sun. There was no time to think as I fought back, wrapping up my attacker in a column of blue magic which he stepped through, three of his friends at his side as the rest fought off my demon and Shaylee's defenses.

This wasn't possible. They shouldn't have been able to

break through my magic, not all three kinds at least. But it was clear whoever they were, they had some kind of augmented power of their own.

Which meant I was in a whole lot of trouble.

Someone roared like a wounded lion from my right side while another voice hissed and spit to my left. I was vaguely aware of Charlotte, her body twisted into half-were form, slashing and spinning her way through my attackers while a ball of silver fur blazed with amber fire, taking on others, but I was alone in the center of the mess with the first vampire and his little friends and had to do something.

We'd only combined our power once before, my demon, Shaylee and I, to protect the Gate from the Unseelie Lord Venner. This time was much easier, though seemed to take forever in the heartbeat I had between the lead vampire's leap and the surge of power I was able to muster.

The twisting column of magics fused at the point into a hammer-head of lime green, slamming directly into the vampire's face. Finally, success, at least partially. The blow flung him backward, to collide with two of his friends as I staggered from the impact myself. Something in him resisted my magic. The blow he took should have spread him over the campus in nice, bite-sized chunks they'd be cleaning up for months. Instead, it simply stunned him.

Not good at all.

And in the rush of the attack, I'd forgotten there were three friends with him. Just as I gathered myself to lash out at the lead vampire again, Charlotte's scream of warning spun me sideways.

"Syd!"

I will be forever grateful for that scream. It gave me just enough time to twist to the side, to avoid the blow meant for my jaw that surely would have crushed my skull, instead only allowing the vampire's hand to brush lightly over my skin, across my chest and over my right hand, now half open as I fought for balance, fingertips momentarily grazing the edge of the virus's prison.

I was blind, vision flooded with so much white light I was certain it would boil my eyes in their sockets. Was I screaming? Had to be, though I barely registered the sound as coming from my throat. The vampire fell back from me, eyes gaping wide, whole body smoking until it suddenly burst into flames. The other vampires fled, shrieking into the night.

None of that mattered as the marble burst and the virus emerged. Not the sound of Charlotte calling my name, not Sassy's desperate cries for help to my mother. Nothing.

Nothing.

The moment the virus escaped it dove into my chest and burrowed itself into my very soul.

Motion surrounded me, voices I knew well: Charlotte, Sassafras. Sashenka's joined them as cool darkness was replaced by light I couldn't see, not while white fire burned through my body, heating my blood, soaking into my cells. My demon snarled and fought, twisting in pain as Shaylee wept and cursed and writhed in her own agony. I couldn't move, no matter the pain, held rigid by the power of the virus.

I knew the exact point when Mom arrived, though I couldn't answer her any more than I could the others. And I felt Gram beside me, fighting with all of her strength, but wasn't able to help.

Frozen, boiling, filled with despair, I gasped one last breath and welcomed it.

Welcomed the moment when my heart stopped.

Why wasn't I surprised she was a she? The virus, her personality, the essence of her, was as female as I was. We stood together in the soft white glow of where ever we were. Some kind of limbo? I couldn't bring myself to care, really. The four of us, points on a compass. My demon reached out to me, thick black nails scratching my wrist before I could take her hand. Shaylee stood on the other side, tall, proud, every inch a Seelie princess though she didn't hesitate to reach for me too.

We can't exist like this. My gaze traveled over the slim, white-haired girl facing me, her transparent skin almost blue, icy eyes cold. *You can't stay here.*

I have nowhere to go. She crossed her arms over her chest. *You've given me no choices, Sydlynn Hayle. When you pulled me out of Sebastian DeWinter, had your demon father lock me inside my prison, he linked you to me as surely as if we'd been made as one.*

My demon growled next to me, bared her teeth. That's what she thought of no choices.

You were killing him, I sent to the virus. No. The vampire essence. I felt her now. Not a disease, an illness. But the very creation of vampires, the very reason for their existence.

Yes, she sent, ignoring my accusation. *You see it now. See me for who I am.*

Created. *By whom?*

The maji. She shook her head, long white hair swinging. *An attempt to perfect humanity. I was a failed experiment by a very idealistic magician. And when she understood I could not do as she needed, she tried to destroy me.*

You fled? I followed her thoughts as she showed me, my

demon and Shaylee along for the ride, soaring as a lonely spirit through time and space.

So alone. She shuddered, held herself, face twisted in grief. *So hungry, in need of what I didn't know. Until I found him.*

Cesard. The Firblog magician she'd struggled with for millennia.

I was certain he would help me. Her sadness twisted to rage. *But he tried to do what the maji wanted, to destroy me and I couldn't let that come to pass. But it was because of him I found it at last, my purpose, what could feed my hunger.*

Blood. I nodded, watched as she fed on peasants, had her first taste, shared her spirit with the very first vampire, a woman who felt familiar to me. The exchange of light, the beauty of it… now I understood.

It's his fault, she sent. *His. I would have been happy to make a family of my own and go no further. But he, in his arrogance, decided it was I who was the enemy, I who was a threat and he began the battle that led me to starve, trapped in a cave with an insane demon lord and the remnants of who Cesard had been.*

Tears trickled down my cheeks as I felt her pain. *I'm sorry. I didn't know.*

And then you trapped me all over again. She shuddered. *I admit, I was lost, broken, when we broke free from our centuries of confinement. I had no soul, no heart, had abandoned all of who I was to hunger and need and isolation. But when I found the vampires you call friends…* she shuddered again, but this time with delight. *I knew at last I could be whole. And Sebastian, he brought me most of the way back.*

Most of the way? I tried not to think of my vampire friend, a wasted husk with only a pair of blue eyes still alive, killing himself to destroy her.

He wasn't meant for me, she sent. *He's already a vampire. Too much of his humanity is lost. And because of that, I was mindless, attempting to fulfill a destiny built into me, but meant to be guided by my consciousness, not allowed to run on the instincts of a blood drinker.*

It was pretty clear what she meant. *You need a host. A human host.*

One with power. She nodded. *And you, with your divided heart, already in three, are perfect.*

And if we try to make you leave? I held my two other sides back by my grips on their hands, though neither made a move to attack her.

You can try. She suddenly looked sad again. *Just for once, I want to belong.*

Okay then. I knew how that felt. *I understand*, I sent. *But we work together, the three of us. Combined, connected. Will you allow us to make you our fourth?*

Her hesitation told me everything I needed to know.

I will consider, she sent. *But for now, please know I mean you no harm. Not unless you try to hurt me.*

Fair warning.

What is it about the power of a heartbeat? A whole lifetime can be lived between one pulse and the next. Or, at least, it felt that way to me.

When I opened my eyes in Mom's quarters, everything came into sharp focus. Her face hovering over mine, fear clear in her blue eyes, the scent of roasted meat mingling with some kind of scented candle burning nearby. The very touch of my clothing was foreign, abrasive in some areas, soft and flexible in others, while the brush of Mom's fingers over my cheek felt like dual paths of fire sending shivers down my spine.

"Syd." Mom's voice was so clear it had edges. How odd. "Sweetheart, how are you feeling?"

Like I'd had some kind of flu? A fainting spell? Her tension hovered around her, anxiety as clear as the glowing blue, green, amber and white aura surrounding her in a shimmering field. How had I never noticed it before?

"I'm fine." And I was. I sat up as I spoke, movements

almost effortless, powerful. She pulled back, sitting next to me as I swung my legs sideways and planted my feet on the dark wood floor. My gaze lifted from the edge of the area rug to settle on Sassafras's amber eyes.

You don't feel all right, he sent.

Well... I took a moment to search around inside myself, found my demon and Shaylee both reasonably content though they did seem a little uncomfortable with our new circumstances. And the essence, the vampire core, sitting quietly in the middle of me, unresisting as I examined her.

An odd peace surrounded me, a calm I'd never felt before. Not only was the whole world, or my perception of it, crisper in every aspect, my troublesome emotions seemed to have been softened somewhat. I prodded the hurt that was Quaid and came up with a bit of sadness, but nothing compared to the fear and longing I'd felt earlier.

What was the vampire doing to me? Was I a vampire myself now? But no, I was certain the moment I considered the possibility that wasn't the case. Not with my demon and Shaylee still in residence. Vampires *were* magic, where as I was still a practitioner.

As much as I probably should have been scared of what was happening, I found myself grinning.

"Cool," I said.

Mom's troubled expression told me she disagreed. "Syd, what happened? Where is the virus?"

She'd noticed it was missing, then. I reached up to touch it out of habit, found the chain gone too. The power of the vampire's release must have dissolved the magic that created it.

"She's not a virus," I said. "And she's inside me."

Multiple gasps almost hurt my ears with the harshness of the sounds. Only then did I look around, though the moment I thought to I already instantly knew exactly who was in the room. Even as my eyes traveled over Erica perched on a chair I felt her, her fear a match to Mom's. Maurice, his horror almost revulsion and I wondered about his prejudice against vampires. Vincent's awe and agreement with me how cool it was and his longing for more magic of his own. But someone was missing, a familiar someone. Had Charlotte abandoned me at last after I ditched her twice?

No. I could feel her then, pacing, panting, furious, frustrated, a room away. Might as well have been a whole continent. I could hear her easily, even from a distance, the churning of her thoughts. Charlotte, flinging herself back and forth the length of the hall near the elevator, locked in a destructive loop of blame and self-hate for allowing me to be hurt.

I ignored everyone, brushed past Sassafras on my way out, shoved aside the door and across the study, flinging the last barrier aside to reach my bodywere. Charlotte froze before her head dropped. She refused to meet my eyes, mouth pulled down into a terrible frown, forehead furrowed in a scowl. There would have been a time I'd have thought she was mad at me, but now I knew differently.

"It's not your fault." No words would heal this. My hand settled on her arm, her skin hotter than I expected as her wolf hovered near the surface, its pain as real as hers. "It's mine." I showed her what I'd done, all of it, kept in a very tight thread, for only the two of us to see. Quaid, my hurt and fear and need. All of it. Her eyes lifted, met mine, the wolf inside her showing herself through the shift in color and intensity for a moment before Charlotte sighed.

"I understand," she said, as I hoped she would. "But don't ever do that to me again." Not an order, not her usual stoic flatness, but with a pleading in her that almost broke my heart.

"I won't," I said. "I promise."

Even though I knew now, without a shadow of a doubt, I'd never need anyone's protection ever again.

Don't get cocky. Gram's mental voice cut through the slowly building euphoria. *You have no idea what this is doing to you.* Even from so far away I could feel her fear through our connection.

Gram, I sent her love and let her touch the calm sitting in the middle of me. *I'm fine. I promise. She's not here to hurt me.*

She better not be. Gram huffed a mental breath. *I love you and would rather you were still around for a while.*

The vampire stirred, but remained silent. Would she speak to me as my demon once had, as Shaylee had brought herself to? Part of me hoped so. There was so much I didn't know yet. And wanted to.

I turned back to Mom, drawing a deep, long breath before letting it out, not wanting to yell at her for almost letting Charlotte self-destruct. "If you would, please." I gestured at the weregirl and Mom actually blushed. A soft touch of power and Charlotte was welcome.

My irritation grew when I realized just how stupid and petty such a welcome was. Still, I needed Mom on my side if I was to walk out of there on my own two feet and not surrounded by Enforcers certain I was a threat. "I'm totally fine, Mom," I said. "Just think of her as one more piece of Syd."

I could tell she wasn't willing to leave it at that. "We have to do a thorough examination," she said, rising to come to my side, magic reaching for me. "To make sure there are no ill effects."

I backed away from her, blocking off her power with a shield burning white. So odd. Why had I called on the vampire's magic? The fragment of undead energy Mom possessed pressed against the barrier, but couldn't break through while the rest of her magic hovered, hesitant.

"Syd, this is the same power that almost killed us, remember?" Erica joined Mom, forming their usual tag-team. When would they learn to trust me?

"That's right," Mom said. "If it hadn't been for Sebastian…"

"Mom." I reached out physically, letting the shield drop, stepping into her space so she could feel me, really feel me. "I'm fine. You know I am."

Her power enveloped me, but didn't try to invade. "You have to give me more than that, sweetheart." I could feel she wanted to believe me, but the pressure of who she was, of who I was, wouldn't allow it. "I have to see for myself."

Why did the idea of my mother's magic exploring inside me make me cringe? It's not like she'd never done it before. But I'd grown so much, learned so much. Taken control of my magic and was stronger for it. Not to mention I'd done things recently I really didn't think she'd want to know about. But, if letting her in was the only way she would trust me, I had no choice.

Not when the alternative was likely being locked up and prodded by witches who studied cases like mine.

Who knew? Maybe that was in my future anyway. But I'd managed to balance my demon and Shaylee so far without calling out the witches with the straightjackets. I had to convince Mom.

I opened up to her, let her inside without reservation. All four of us did, even the vampire, much to my relief.

If this is the only way we can continue to function, she sent to me while Mom examined us, *I am willing to do anything*.

Except leave. So she would be able to talk to me. Even as I spoke I knew I didn't want her to.

Except that, yes. She was smiling.

Mom finally pulled away, shaking a little as she pressed one hand to her heart. "You are fine," she whispered, voice hoarse. "More than fine." Why was she afraid? "I've never felt anything like it in my life. And it," she paused, "she, is completely different than she was when we fought Cesard."

"I told you." I hugged myself on impulse, feeling the strength of my powers and my body like I'd been given a massive gift. "It's awesome."

Mom's shaky laugh had a hopeless edge. "We still need to have you examined more closely."

Straightjacket time. Lovely.

"But," she went on, "I see no reason why you can't continue as normal, as long as you feel all right."

"Miriam." Mom's name was a gasp from Erica's throat.

Mom shook her head. "No matter what's happened, Syd is in full control. Which means I trust her to let me know the moment anything might change." Spoken to Erica but meant for me.

Got it, loud and clear.

Mom ushered everyone into the waiting elevator, just as Meira crept in from a side door and rushed to me to hug me.

"I was worried, but Mom didn't want me in here." She looked up at me, amber eyes full of tears. "Are you okay?"

I hugged her back, kissed her cheek. "I'm fantastic," I whispered in her ear. "Let me take care of this and I'll tell you all about it."

She nodded, pulled away with a little smile as I followed her into the sitting room and took a seat on the edge of the sofa while Mom paced the room, long skirt brushing over Sassafras's twitching tail on every pass.

"I mean it, Syd," she said as she walked, head down,

forehead bunched. "The instant something changes I want to know about it." She stopped, turned to me with a hopeless expression. "You realize I should have you locked up? That there will be those on the Council who demand I do?"

"You can try." My demon rumbled her anger, Shaylee indignant, but the vampire inside me simply observing, her quiet calm a great comfort. "There's nothing wrong with me. If anything, things are better than they were before. And you know very well I'm capable of balancing this."

She sighed, ran one hand over her face. "If anyone is," she said. "You've had a lifetime of training." Mom's arms dropped to her sides, her face sad. "Just… be careful. We have no idea if she has an agenda."

The vampire stirred at that, as though she wanted to defend herself, and I paused, listened. But she didn't speak up or argue, just settled again.

"I promise," I said, "if anything happens, you'll be the first to know. But I don't want you to worry. I have lots of protection, remember?" I tapped my temple with one finger. "Not just my demon and Shaylee, I have Gram in here with me. And Charlotte and Sassafras watching my outside." I closed the distance between us and hugged Mom, letting her feel how much I loved her. All of our coldness and the tension between us melted in that moment and for the first time since she'd left Wilding Springs to take over as Council Leader she was just my mom.

"I love you so much," she whispered in my ear. "I just want to keep you safe. And I've done a terrible job of that." She pushed me back, apology on her face before she even spoke. "I didn't look into the issue you brought to me and clearly that was a mistake. The vampires who attacked you may have come from the Star Club."

"Makes the most logical sense." Sassafras's growl was accompanied by a thrash of his tail, though I knew he wasn't angry with Mom or me but with himself. I was surrounded by people who blamed themselves for everything. No wonder I did it too.

"I'll send Enforcers over immediately," she said. "But for now I want you to stay here tonight."

I shook my head immediately. "I'm going back to my dorm," I said. "And my life."

She hesitated, hands still holding my arms but I gently, oh-so-gently, pulled free of her.

"Mom," I said. "I love you too. But I have to go."

I turned away from her before she could protest and went to hug Meira again.

"I'll be back tomorrow," I said. "Promise."

Meira clung to me a moment before letting me go first. "Okay," she said. "Night, Syd."

I had the best sister ever.

I wasn't surprised when Charlotte practically took my arm on the walk back to my dorm, nor by the feeling of watchers dressed in black robes who observed us as we made our way the very short distance back to my hall. It was almost funny, actually, but my weregirl companion wasn't laughing and neither were the Enforcers who stood guard, so I held in my amusement.

The feeling that everything was sharper and clearer had begun to fade, as was my ability to feel and almost see the emotions of those around me. I found myself missing the intimacy of it though had to admit it would make life more complicated if I was constantly distracted by the emotions of others. Still it was nice to have insights I'd never had before and understand with absolute clarity I wasn't the only one who was screwed up.

Sassafras trotted at my side, refusing to let me carry him. "Just in case," he said. And he might have been right. The precious second it would take me to drop him if we were attacked could make a difference. Then again, with three Enforcers, Charlotte and him guarding over me for the minute it took me to walk from Mom's place to my hall, his caution really seemed like overkill.

Sashenka opened the door just as Charlotte grasped for the knob, her face pale under her lovely dark tone.

"Syd!" She pulled me into the room, ignoring Charlotte who allowed it, though I knew if the weregirl hadn't trusted Sashenka, my roommate would be flat on her back and out cold by now. "Everyone is talking about what happened. Well," she rolled her eyes with a soft huff of breath, "us witches anyway. We all saw the light, felt the vampires." Her eyes were huge. "Enforcers were everywhere wiping normal's memories and sending us all back to our dorms."

I sighed and shrugged. Yet another reason for my fellow witch students to alienate me. Whatever.

"I'm fine," I said, suddenly tired. "Honest."

She sank onto her bed with a big smile of relief. "You look fine," she said. "Phew! I was really worried. And those vampires." Sashenka shuddered a little. "What were they doing in the Yard? Everyone knows they're not allowed."

It wasn't until she mentioned it my mind went back to the attack and the odd way the vampires were able to reach through my magic. Yes, their power had different properties, but there was no way they should have been able to defeat all three kinds of my magic at once.

Unless they had help. Which made me think of Darin and his witch and vampire warded club.

"I'm sure the Enforcers will find out," I said, frowning at Charlotte as she pulled open the door of my wardrobe and jerked out a spare pillow and blanket. "What are you doing?"

She didn't meet my eyes, just spread the quilt out on the floor beside my bed. "You know exactly what I'm doing," she said.

Just great. And even though I knew it wasn't necessary, I didn't have the heart to kick her out.

Sashenka frowned a little, though not in anger, just curiosity before shrugging. "I heard stuff like this happened around you," she said with a giggle, "but I had no idea being your roommate would mean I'd get to witness it."

Oh yeah, hardy-har-har. "Be careful what you wish for."

Sashenka didn't get a chance to answer. The moment I spoke, someone knocked on the door and she rose quickly to answer it.

I couldn't have been more shocked to see Mia standing in the hallway on the other side.

She didn't greet my roommate or even look at her, instead

shoving her way past Sashenka to come to stand in the middle of the room, ice blue eyes locked on me.

"We need to talk," she said, voice as cold as her gaze. "Coven leader to coven leader."

Even Charlotte took the hint, though reluctantly, leaving after the blushing Sashenka, pulling the door most of the way closed, but enough of a crack remaining I could see her standing on the other side like an immovable wall.

Only Sassafras remained, curled up on my pillow, amber eyes watching carefully as Mia dissolved from her stiff arrogance into a mess of sobbing.

Um. What?

"It's so hard!" Her wail was loud enough I winced, my more sensitive hearing still affecting me. "I thought I could handle it, could do what Mother wanted." She looked up at me from where she'd pressed her face into her hands, streaks of black makeup tracking down her pale cheeks, expression so desperate I wanted to hug her and rock her like she was my little sister after a nightmare. "But I can't do it, Syd, I can't. They won't listen to me."

The Dumont family. I'd worried about her from day one, when she took control of the nastiest coven on the continent. Mia had never been strong to begin with, so the idea of her being a coven leader, of turning things around when most of the family was probably pretty happy continuing to be assholes if the brothers were any indication, was ridiculous.

What was Mom thinking? Oh, right. Mom wasn't Council Leader when Mia took the job. And likely she wouldn't have been able to do anything anyway. Covens were autonomous when it came to their rule.

Stupid, in my opinion.

Then again, the last thing I'd want would be the Council poking around my coven's business, so I supposed the rules were there for a reason.

Get out of your own crap and pay attention. Gram's harsh tone snapped me out of my thoughts. *This is important, Syd. We have an opportunity here.*

Sigh. *The war is over, Gram, remember? Odette is dead.* The former leader of the Dumonts had died at Mom's trial, killed by Batsheva Moromond as the blood witch fled her attempt to take over the Council. Yes, Gram had lots of reason to hate the family, but her main goal was accomplished.

The woman who had been behind all of the hurt in Gram's adult life was gone.

Don't be a fool. Gram's mental voice cuffed me. *The Dumonts will never stop, not until their evil is weeded out. Generations of it, Syd. Now pay attention.*

She'd spent my whole life telling me the same thing. Probably a good idea to listen.

I gathered up my resolve and took Mia's arm, guiding her to my bed and sitting beside her with one arm around her shoulders.

"You're stronger than you think," I said, handing her a tissue. "I know it. And so do they."

She shook her head while she noisily blew her nose. "They know I'm weak," she whispered, staring down at the wad of dirty tissue in her hands. "I've been doing my best, keeping up the act. But there's just so much corruption… I issue orders and they find ways around them, loopholes. They talk around me, confuse me, make me feel stupid." Mia snuffled. "I need help."

Perfect. Gram's nasty chortle actually made me angry.

She's my friend, I snapped.

She's a Dumont, Gram growled back. *You're a coven leader, like it or not. Act like one.*

Mumble, grumble.

"What about Quaid?" A ping of pain fired off in my heart. Whatever the vampire inside me had done to dull the ache was wearing off as well. Crappy. Still, it helped to focus on Mia. And Quaid was strong, no doubt about it. If she would reach out to him, have him at her side, the coven would be more likely to listen.

One thing about Quaid, he could see right through bull.

Mia sighed deeply, shoulders slumping. "He's too busy with the Enforcer trainees he's made friends with," she said. I recognized the petulance in her voice. Had used that same tone myself in the past.

Swore I never would again if that was how it made me sound.

Never.

"I know he'd help if you asked him." Or did I? Quaid did seem lost in his own stuff lately. The jerk.

Yeah, that was better. Pain turned to anger. Jerk. Jerky jerk-jerkified jerkwad.

Syd. Gram tapped at the edges of my mind, her words dry. *Hello.*

Right.

Mia's desperate gaze met mine. "I trust you," she said. "Like no one else. You're the only one who can help me, I just know it." She broke down into tears again, hugging me around the neck, whole body shaking so hard the steel rings on her heavy leather belt tapped together like chiming bells. "Please help me."

"Of course I will." I shoved Gram aside even as Sassafras crossed my lap and into Mia's. She let me go, stroking his soft fur as he purred so loudly my jaw ached. His demon magic slid around her and calmed her down to the point she was able to blow her nose again and swipe at the black tracks on her cheeks without bursting into more tears.

"You are leader," Sassafras said. "They must obey you. Yours is the power that feeds the family magic."

She nodded, black-lipsticked mouth turned down. "I know," she said. "But even when I threaten to take the power away they just ignore me, and when I catch them doing things they shouldn't, they find reasons around my orders."

Gram reached through me, linked to Mia. I saw my friend's eyes widen when my grandmother spoke up.

Are you leader, or aren't you?

Mia stuttered a moment before nodding.

Are you or aren't you? I didn't like Gram's tone one bit, nor the way she was prodding Mia.

Showed what I knew. The harder Gram pushed, the madder Mia got until she shouted in all of our minds.

I AM THE LEADER OF THE DUMONT COVEN.

Okay then.

Then act like it. Gram's mental voice softened. *Sometimes you have to wield a sword to get the job done, but girl, you have to be willing to use it. And if they think you won't, if they feel you hesitate even for a second, you've told them you can't do what it takes. Do you understand?*

Mia nodded, miserable now, the anger running out of her. "I do," she whispered.

"Time to clean house," Sassafras said so matter-of-factly Mia locked eyes with him. "Ethpeal is totally correct. Cut a few of the worst trouble makers loose and the rest will fall into line."

She gaped at him. "I can't do that."

Yes, Gram sent. *You can. And you must. They have to take you seriously. Right now they don't. But strip a half a dozen or so and send them packing and you have your control back.*

Mia shook harder, hands trembling as she stroked Sassy's fur. "But how?" She met my eyes, hers welling with fear and tears. "They won't leave."

"They won't have a choice," Sassafras said, "if they have no power left."

I could see my friend's body unbend, her spine straightening as she thought it through. "Cut them off," she whispered. "Get rid of them."

"That's right," I said. "Without the worst of them around, life will be much easier. And you'll be in a better position to straighten out the coven."

Mia actually smiled then, a small smile, but she was no longer shaking and the two very bright spots of pink on her cheeks were fading as she pulled herself under control.

"How?" She was still looking at me, but hope had blossomed in her eyes.

"Don't give them a chance to argue with you." Sassafras stood, paws on her shoulders so she was forced to look in his eyes. "And don't do a big group all at once."

Single them out, in private. Gram's growl was hungry. *Cut them lose when they are in a weak position. Don't ever let them rally support before you cut them off.*

Mia was nodding, but frowning too. "Won't that make me seem, I don't know, cowardly?"

Gram snorted. *Better that than a puppet leader run roughshod by her coven.*

Mia's face tightened with determination. "You're right," she said. "There will be time for bravery later."

"It will take all of your strength to do this," Sassy said. "But you're not alone. Find those in your coven who will stand with you and draw on them for support."

Mia hugged him suddenly before releasing him to hug me, too.

Thank you, she sent to all of us, even Gram.

Go talk to Miriam, Gram said. *Tell her what you're planning, as a courtesy.*

"So she can warn the other covens not to welcome those witches." Sassy hopped over me and settled on my pillow again. "Powerless, they will serve as the perfect example."

Mia leaped to her feet, cheeks flushed again, but this time with happiness. "I knew coming to you was the right choice." She smiled, a real smile before rushing out the door.

I sank back to my bed as Charlotte entered, face a cold mask. I'm sure she heard everything, except the mental bits, but would have caught enough to get the picture.

Do you think she'll go through with it? Sassy's mental voice addressed both Gram and I.

I was about to answer yes when Gram sighed. *Doubtful,* she sent, tired and frustrated. *Mia's mother didn't do her any favors cutting off her power for so long.*

I seem to recall someone else in a similar position. I didn't mean to shoot back at Gram, but I wanted to defend my friend.

You're different, girl, Gram growled. *You're a Hayle. I've never worried about your ability to lead.*

I agree with Ethpeal, Sassy sent. *Mia is simply too damaged, too weak. Without a support system in place, she's doomed to fail.*

At least Miriam is aware and has been watching her. Gram's mental touch lightened a little, but not much as I wondered how much my mother and grandmother talked business while leaving me out of it. *It's a touchy situation all around. The girl is stubborn and yet doesn't have the power to step up and do what she must. And as much as the Dumonts have fallen out of favor,* she sounded like that gave her great satisfaction, *they are still a powerful coven requiring a firm hand.*

Maybe we've changed that? I bit back the bitterness of knowing Gram and Mom still didn't trust me enough to tell me everything.

Perhaps. Sassy sighed. *I doubt it. Is there a contingency plan in place, Ethpeal?*

What did he mean by that? Gram grunted softly.

Miriam's dealing with it, she sent. *No matter what happens, the Dumont coven won't remain leaderless if the girl finally collapses.*

Covens are autonomous, I sent, a little horrified by the implication. The Council wasn't meant to interact on that level. *Mom can't interfere.* Could she?

Just keep an eye on your friend, Gram sent. *And we'll see where things go.*

The loyal friend in me wanted to argue, but knowing Mia the way I did, I just couldn't muster anything in her defense.

27

It was a weird thing to me, the next morning, thinking about going to class. Like everything was fine and nothing had changed. But things *had* changed.

The strangest dreams plagued me all night, tied to the vampire and her history—the ancient people she encountered, her battles with Cesard. And though I woke completely rested and feeling like I'd slept for a week rather than just a few hours, I'd finally found my worry button.

Every time I tried to think about her, though, I found myself instead focusing on Quaid or the attacking vampire problem. How much control did she have and was she able to deflect my thoughts?

As I crossed the Yard on my way to breakfast, Sashenka chattering away beside me, Charlotte hovering so close I was sure she'd walk on the back of my shoe at any second, I reached inside with purpose and touched the vampire.

Listen, I sent, *I know we've gotten on along well so far, but stop messing with my thoughts or you'll find yourself behind a shield.*

She bristled a little, prickly but still calm. *It's wasteful for you to fret over me*, she sent back. *I'm simply pointing you toward things that are more important.*

I'll decide what's important, I snapped back. *This is my life, my body. Remember that.*

She paused. *No, Sydlynn. This is our life, our body. All of us.*

Didn't help that my demon and Shaylee actually took her side.

Bad enough dealing with my own crap. The last thing I needed was my multiple personalities staging a takeover coup.

I know that, I sent back to all of them. *But we have to find some harmony here. And as it happens, I'm the one in charge. Okay?*

My demon grumbled her agreement while Shaylee sighed and did the same. But the vampire just shrugged, an act that made me shudder all over.

If this is to work, there must be a leader, she admitted. *But it remains to be seen if you are capable of such leadership.*

Um, hello?

You know what? I wrapped witch magic around her, the

inner layer of spirit. *Just for now let's treat this like a trial period, okay? You can watch all you want, and I won't try to kick you out and seal you up permanently.* Since I had no idea if that was even possible, I was just bluffing, but it was the best I could do. *But if you do anything at all to make me act or try to take me over, this cooperation thing is done. Get me?*

She backed off immediately, surprising me a little. I was sure she was prepped for a fight.

I'm sorry, she sent. *You're correct. Until you've proven yourself to me, I will remain an observer.*

I still didn't like what she was saying, but at least I hadn't triggered Sydageddon.

Worked for me.

Aside from Liam, Sashenka and the girls—a little wide-eyed themselves as they peppered me with questions over breakfast—the majority of the student body continued to ignore me. Only now, instead of being resentful, they seemed afraid.

Was that an improvement? Hard to tell. But I'd take it.

Every time I prodded Mom for information about the Star Club and the vampires she brushed me off with an, "I'm handling it," or cut me off all together. Yeah, I just bet she was handling it. Which meant she hadn't found anything and had decided either I was wrong about Darin and his little secret society or someone had convinced her the vampire attack was some single aberration now done with.

I finally tracked down Rupe and Simon crossing the Yard on their way to class, determined to get some answers from them at least, only to have them stonewall me.

"Some of us are trying to fit in," Rupe snapped.

"With someone like Darin?" I wasn't in the mood to go easy on them. Not when it was likely said witch had something to do with the attack on me the night before. "You two really want to be friends with someone like him?"

I should have known the devil in question wasn't far away. The moment the words passed my lips Darin appeared with his typical two-witch posse, grinning at me with eyes half-lidded like he'd heard what I said.

Like I cared.

I wasn't expecting his magic to slam into my shields so hard I staggered back a step before I recovered.

"Watch your step, Syd," Darin said, flicking his fingers at me as if I was inconsequential.

"You watch yours." I was so ready for a fight. So. Ready. He was about to learn what it was like to push me around. "Thought I taught you this lesson already."

Crap. Simon and Rupe were looking at us like they were

totally confused and we were in a very public place. What was I thinking?

Darin didn't seem to be held back by such issues. "You have no idea who you're dealing with," he hissed at me, stepping forward to poke me in the chest with one finger. Just barely. The moment he touched me, Charlotte had his hand in hers and twisted so violently he fell to his knees with a cry of pain. Didn't care, not even a little.

He. Touched. Me.

Oh no he did *not*.

My demon roared, surging into my eyes. I stepped in, pulling Charlotte from him, even as my witch magic drove into his solar plexus. I didn't shred his shields this time, instead used them as a battering ram, my power pushing so hard his own wards slammed into him. He was just regaining his feet when I struck, making him curse and stagger back, almost falling again, only to have his two lackeys catch him.

"Don't. Ever. Touch. Me." I didn't need to see Charlotte to know she was ready to kill him, and had I not intervened he'd likely have stopped breathing by now. I'd saved his stupid damned life even while part of me wished I'd let her tear him into tiny bits.

"Just keep pushing, Syd," Darin snarled as he straightened,

snapping his fingers at my friends who rose immediately and fell in behind him. "See where it gets you next time we catch you alone."

He was part of the attack. Didn't have to say anything else—I could see it in his eyes, in the hate he aimed at me. And his parting remark told me everything I needed to know.

I watched him go, longing to chase him down, but knowing without more solid proof than some vague threat Mom wouldn't listen.

Besides, I had class. Yeah, exactly where I wanted to be. Especially with Liam and Sashenka sitting close together, laughing and talking like they were old friends, leaving me out of it. More jealousy, really, Syd? Seemed to be a cycle with me.

I took the time to think about Quaid, really think about him and what I'd done. What we'd done. Even as I gently felt along the connection between us, finding it mostly blocked off, only the faintest impressions of him, happy, laughing, without me, regret filled me.

I'd given him everything I had, my heart and body and soul. Thought he'd done the same. How could I have been so stupid? He was an eighteen-year-old guy, more screwed up than I was. Of course he hadn't turned me down when I'd... sigh.

Idiot.

Gram's mental touch was gentle, but her words were harsh.

I warned you, she sent. *He's a Dumont, Syd. Remember that.*

Maybe it was rude to cut her off, but I wasn't really in the mood for I told you so.

28

I lasted the entire day without actually contacting Quaid, a fact of which I was very proud. No needy, grasping me. Nope, nope.

It was hard to maintain that stance when I finally reached for him only for Quaid to gently tell me he couldn't talk and cut me off.

Jerkaroni.

Didn't help I felt her in his background. The honey-blonde. Whatever her stupid name was.

Didn't help at all.

I peeled away from the gang and went my own way, sitting in a quiet corner of the cafeteria alone with Charlotte to eat my dinner, calling up as much anger as I could to keep from going in search of Quaid and demanding he love me.

Jerkasaurus.

My aloneness continued with a short walk through the Yard to the Holden Chapel where I found a bench between two large, sheltering bushes and sat on my hands to keep from wringing them together. The sound of mingling voices, the glee choir singing inside the chapel, helped to calm me a little. It was something to focus on at least and they really were very, very good.

I had only a moment's warning, a twitch inside my chest telling me something was coming, before Alison appeared in a streak of glowing white and dove straight for me.

Maybe if her face hadn't been twisted into deathly rictus, I might not have acted. But there was so much hate in her my reaction was instant and violent, magic surging forward to block her. When the echo of her slammed into the barrier, she howled an unearthly sound that silenced the choir for a moment before they went on, a little breathless from fright.

But didn't come to check. Thanks to the magic on campus. Freaky.

"GIVE IT TO ME!" Alison's shrill scream was no longer audible to normal ears, I made sure of that. I let my power wrap her up, like a ghostly sausage in a blanket, even as she raged at me. "I can feel it inside you, Syd. It's mine, not yours and I want it NOW!"

She flung herself at my shields, sliding through parts of the energy only to become trapped as I poured more magic into the webbing.

"Alison, stop." I lurched to my feet, Charlotte on guard, but knowing there was nothing she could do to help. "That's enough."

"It's NOT." She squirmed and fought and clawed toward me. "Give me my life back!"

Back? "Don't you dare blame me for dying," I shot at her. "You killed yourself."

Oh no. Did I really just say that out loud?

Alison's wail almost drove me to my knees, not because of the sound, but because I knew I'd finally reached her.

"I DIDN'T." She stopped fighting. "I didn't kill myself." I watched her as she almost panted with the effort. "I didn't, Syd."

"Yes," I said, softly, gently. She had to accept the truth. Maybe if she did it would help her move on. "Alison, you were drunk and upset and you drove your car into the lake and you drowned."

She shook her head with violence. "I would never."

"You would." I sighed. "You did. The night in the kitchen. With the butcher knife. You cut your artery, Alison. You tried to kill yourself then." I'd saved her while her mother watched in terror, my demon's magic sealing the wound with amber fire. But Alison would have died, bled out, if Angela Morgan hadn't called me to come and save her daughter.

She gaped at me in pure horror, the blue of her eyes going very wide before flooding with black.

"Nonononononono." She jerked once, actually pulling free of the net of power I had around her, but didn't try to attack me again so I let her hover there before me, lost in her own grief and suffering. "I didn't. Did I?" The last came out in a little girl voice. I wished I could hug her, tell her it was all right, but it wasn't all right.

Would never be again.

She has to be destroyed. Gram's voice was soft, but firm. *Syd, you can't let her go on like this. Think of your friend, the one you loved. Now look at this shadow of who she's becoming.*

I know. I reached out to the echo of my friend, gathering my magic. *I wish it could be different.*

But Alison acted faster than I could. She lunged away from me, as if sensing I was about to capture her again. She rose from the ground, hovering over me, eyes still black, face drooping almost as if she was a partially melted candle.

"You'll pay for betraying me," she hissed. "I'll have my revenge, Sydlynn Hayle. I'll have my revenge!"

She flashed out of view, gone. I reached out, tried to track her, but she was out of contact, even when I used the new and unfamiliar connection with the vampire in the hope the power Alison stole would make her easier to find.

Nothing.

You have to track her, Gram sent. *And destroy her.*

Agreed. The vampire's voice made Gram twitch a little, but she didn't comment. *That ghost echo cannot be permitted to exist this way, not with the power she stole from me feeding her. The need for more, like the need for blood, will drive her mad until she is only a monster.*

So that was it. *She's craving blood?*

Possibly. The vampire thought a moment. *If she is able to find a way to feed... I don't know if she's considered it yet, if she's figured out what she really craves. It sounds like she hasn't. But if she does, I have no idea what she will become.*

She won't be able to feed, I said. *She's an echo.*

With form and substance, thanks to the vampire virus. Gram's tone was so grim I didn't correct her terminology. *Remember that, Syd. She's not Alison anymore.*

No, the vampire agreed. *She's much more than that. But,* she went on, *we have more important things to worry about at the moment.*

What do you mean? I turned to Charlotte who scowled into the trees around us, noticing how dark it had become.

We're not alone, she said.

29

I reached out with my magic immediately, even as I pulled my shields around me and prepared to fight. The essence's calm helped me stay focused, even as we tracked the three vampires who almost crossed our path, only a few yards further ahead past the trees, on their way across the Yard toward my dorm.

Or, at least, heading in that direction. Assuming they were after me was a leap, though not a big one.

"Come on." I took off at a run, Charlotte beside me, heading for the trio of white power I felt sliding through the early night ahead of me. Why were they corporeal? They could just as easily have shuddered into darkness and traveled that way. Why risk being exposed?

I paused behind one of the large trees at the edge of the Yard and had my answer.

Rupe. Simon. Three vampires. Leading them away.

Oh *hell* no.

But before I could reach them, before I do anything,

the vampires latched onto my friends and did their disappearing act.

Taking the boys with them.

I pounded to a halt only a moment later in the place they had just been, a million swear words bubbling in my head as I spun in a frustrated circle, focus falling on the path the boys had always taken to the club house.

The moment I reached for Charlotte she took my hand without question, sliding into the veil beside me for the quick ride to Holyoke. The vamps weren't the only ones with the means to travel.

We arrived too late, just in time to see Rupe and Simon disappear through the front door with the vampires behind them. The last one paused, turned, long black leather coat swinging around his feet. Grinned at me. I knew him, the same one who touched the marble containing the power I now carried within me, the vampire who broke through my shields and tried to kill me.

Closed the door behind him.

That one's mine, the vampire said.

Done. I turned to Charlotte. "Now we know things are hinky over there," I said.

"And why they so quickly abandoned your friendship." Charlotte snarled. "I should have sensed it."

"They aren't under thrall," I said. "I felt for that."

"Not to witches," Charlotte said. "To the vampires."

They were... what? "They've been feeding from my friends?" Oh, it made so much sense now. No wonder I hadn't felt it, I wasn't looking for it. And for someone like Rupe who had his head on his shoulders... okay, Simon I could see going over to the dark side out of a need to fit in, but Rupe? No way.

"So freaking illegal," I whispered.

"I'm sorry," Charlotte said. "I should have sensed it."

"You weren't meant to." I promised myself I'd kill Darin the moment I saw him again. "The witches are hiding it."

What were they doing? Whatever it was, it was making both magicks stronger, both camps adopting parts of each other's power. Not a far-fetched idea, considering everyone living inside me, or the fact my mother still had parts of various kinds of magic at her disposal thanks to Batsheva's attempt to take over my coven.

Was I that big of an idiot I thought no one else would try it too?

"We have to tell your mother." Charlotte held out her hand.

You have to act. Gram's voice cut through my agreement with the weregirl.

What? I froze, almost touching Charlotte. *Mom has to deal with this.*

You've already told your mother, Gram said, *and she's done nothing.*

True, but—

Listen to me, girl. Gram's voice grated over mine, her anger obvious, but not at me. At Mom. *Your mother won't act. Can't. Think about it. You were attacked by vampires. And what has she done?*

Nothing. Gram—

Her hands are tied, Gram sent. *But yours aren't. You are a coven leader, Sydlynn Hayle, and you have every right, under the witch's charter, to defend yourself.*

I drew a deep breath. Right.

Awesome.

Was it wrong I was suddenly excited by the idea?

I let my hand drop. "We have to do something," I said. "And now that I know the vampires who attacked me are in that house, I'm in my rights to do so."

Charlotte's hesitation lasted no longer than it took for the wolf inside her to surge into her eyes.

"I'm in," she said, accent rough as her own need to act got the better of her.

"But we need help first," I said. "Give me a second."

I reached immediately for Sassafras. *I found the vampires.*

You what? I could feel him moving, running, sliding through the veil himself until by the time the echo of his words faded from my mind he appeared at my feet in a flash of amber fire. "Where?" He looked around, eyes settling on the clubhouse. "You're sure?"

"We both saw them," I said. "And I recognized them."

He nodded slowly. "I'll go tell your mother."

"No," I said. "We're taking care of this. She's had her shot."

Sassy paused. "You're sure you want to do this?"

"I'm a coven leader," I said. "What else do you expect me to do?"

He sighed heavily, bowed his head. But when he looked up again, his eyes burned. "I'm at your command."

Wow. Holy.

Okay then.

"There's one more person I want to talk to first." I almost reached for Liam mentally then froze. Why Liam? Shouldn't my first thought have been Quaid? After all, he had access to a whole class full of Enforcer trainees and Liam was just one person.

But it all went to trust, didn't it? Still, I had to give Quaid the chance to redeem himself. No more Miss Nice Syd.

No more waiting for him to get his act together, to figure out what he really wanted. This wasn't some heart breaking moment I was dealing with. Things were getting serious and either he was in or he was out.

The veil delivered Charlotte and me in the Yard, Sassy left behind to watch the club house. Not a peep from Mom, at least, not like it would have mattered. I stormed my way into Quaid's dorm, feeling for him as I went, finding him in the common room with a crowd of other students.

Quaid. I cracked my power like a whip. *We need to talk.*

The scowl on his face told me I'd taken the wrong approach, but I really didn't give a crap. He hadn't believed me before. He was about to get an education in listening when Syd talked.

The honey-blonde hovered near him, but held back when he stormed across the room and tried to grab my arm, to steer me away. Nope, not having any. I let him have my power full in the chest, knocking him backward, letting him feel the coven leader in me.

Quaid flinched, flushed. He clearly assumed I was there because I was jealous. The need to laugh in his face was almost unbearable, tied up with the grief in my heart telling me things weren't going to turn out well between us after all.

"I need your help." I filled him in on the details, using my power to show him exactly what happened. Including the vampire attack the night before. He reacted with guilt. So he knew I'd been in trouble and hadn't come to find out if I was okay?

King of Jerkistan.

When I wrapped up with what I'd just discovered, I paused. "Think you and your Enforcer friends are up to helping out?"

Quaid took a half step back. "You need to tell your mother," he said. "The Council has to handle this. And the enlisted Enforcers."

"I tried that, twice." I stood there, arms crossed over my chest, fury growing as the coward in him showed his ugly face. Really Quaid? Really?

So that was how it was going to be.

His one last moment of hesitation was all I needed. I punched him hard with a ball of power, making him grunt and clutch his stomach, dark eyes meeting mine, full of his own pain and a whole world of regret. Yeah, he could cry me a river.

"Thanks for having my back," I said. "See you around, Quaid. Hope your little girlfriend is worth it."

I left him there, letting my rage wash through me,

snapping at my demon who hummed her unhappiness as I left him behind.

Screw that. He'd shown me who he really was at last. And I was done.

Liam it was. If he was even still talking to me.

I'd barely reached his door, hand raised to knock, when Liam jerked it open.

"Syd," he said, face full of concern, "what's wrong?"

Was I really broadcasting that much? Oops. Time to tone it back a little bit. But my encounter with Quaid had me riled up and I'd done nothing but stew over it my entire stomping journey to Liam's door.

"I need your help." Part of me cringed, waiting for him to abandon me too.

"Anything." He grabbed his jacket, was out the door and standing beside me before I could recover from the surge of gratitude that went a long way to healing the mess Quaid left behind. I hugged him hard, welcoming the earthy feeling of his Sidhe power and was even more thankful when Liam hugged me back.

"Thank you for trusting me," I whispered.

"Always," he said. Pushed me back. "I tried to see you last night, after the attack." His face twisted in concern. "But Charlotte and your mother wouldn't let me."

I glanced at my bodywere who had the good grace to look embarrassed.

"You needed your rest," she said.

Yeah. Right. "Being over protective again?"

She shrugged but at least she was smiling.

"Then today..." he hesitated, as if he felt like he owed me an explanation, but didn't want to say it.

"Liam, it's okay," I said.

"No," he shook his head, blonde hair throwing glints of red in the light of the hall. "It's not. I was angry with you, and worried, and... well, worried mostly. I didn't know what to say to you. About Quaid."

My heart froze. Did my Sidhe friend know what I'd done?

"Liam—"

"You're a big girl," he growled. "You can take care of yourself. I have to keep reminding myself it's not my job to protect you."

I hugged him again, more gently. "Thank you for always being here for me."

He nodded into my hair. "Now, tell me where we're going and who we're planning to take down."

My Liam. The best ever.

So why couldn't Quaid step up like that?

A quick ride on the veil later and the four of us, my demon cat huddled at my feet, looked out over the street and at the quiet Star Club house, each of us using our power to try to break through the wards while Charlotte kept a look out for approaching members.

Liam shook his head at last. I'd hoped his Sidhe power, untouched by witch magic, would be able to find a work around the wards, but it was clear from the disappointed frown on his face he'd failed.

As had I, despite the help I had from my demon, Shaylee and the vampire. Mind you, I knew I could have smashed my way through them, no problem. But sneaking in, that would be much harder. And I wasn't really ready to show my hand just yet.

Not without some very specialized backup.

"Okay," I said, "Plan B."

"Which is?" Sassafras's fur was fluffed to its full extension, making him look like a very soft silver cloud, punctuated by two angry demon eyes.

I didn't bother answering him. I was too busy reaching for Sebastian.

31

The moment Sebastian's mind touched mine, he hissed in concern.

Sydlynn, he sent. *What's happened?*

I filled him in as fast as I could, telling him about the vampire attack.

And the touch was enough to shatter the virus's prison? Sebastian's sympathy was powerful, as was his doubt and curiosity. *But you are you yet, I can feel it. How is this possible?*

Because I'm whole again, the vampire told him. *Thanks to you, Sebastian.*

Another rapid conversation, and while Sebastian's concern faded somewhat, he didn't completely release it.

I would like to spend more time speaking with both of you, he sent. *But for now, you're correct. This situation takes precedence. You believe this clan is feeding from your friends?* He paused, considered. I didn't argue, just enjoying the silkiness of his mind. I'd always had a girl-crush on

Sebastian, even his mental touch full of deliciousness I had to shield against so he wouldn't feel it.

Embarrassing enough, I still woke from the odd dream seeing him standing in the courtroom with only his shredded clothing to cover certain... bits.

Bad girl, Syd. Naughty thoughts were for later.

It's impossible for me to know what clan they come from at this distance. He hesitated one more moment before his power slid over me like a caress, though I'm certain he meant it kindly and not in the way my body took it. Seemed my little exploration with Quaid had woken a whole lot of things I wasn't sure I was prepared for. Sebastian either didn't sense my reaction or chose, kindly, to ignore it. *I'll send help,* he sent. *And we'll get to the bottom of this. Well done, witch girl.*

I missed him when he left me with one last touch.

Syd! Focus.

I rubbed at my bright red cheeks, grateful for the darkness surrounding us while the others stared at me.

"Sorry," I said. "We should have visitors short—"

The air shuddered and two vampires shifted out of the black to appear beside us. But these two I had no hesitation in hugging, the warmth of their bodies telling me they'd eaten.

"Uncle Frank." I kissed his perfect cheek, smiling into his handsome face, the one I remembered. Gone was the scarring left behind by his exposure to the sun, done at the orders of Odette and the arrangement of Ameline. When Uncle Frank served as the gateway between me and Sebastian when we'd removed the vampire essence, her touch had healed my uncle and brought him all the way back to us.

His smile was so dear I wanted to hug him again but, pressed for time, I instead turned and latched onto his gorgeous girlfriend, Sunny. She whispered her love in my ear as I let her presence fill me up with as much confidence as I'd ever felt.

Nothing like having those who really, really loved me by my side when I needed them.

It wasn't until I set her loose they both drew a breath into lungs that didn't need to breathe and stared at me like I was some kind of alien.

Clearly Sebastian didn't have time to fill them in, just told them to come. And they did. No questions asked.

Yup, I was one lucky girl.

Another fast conversation, this time with help from Charlotte, Liam and Sassy, and the two vampires were frowning, grim, but nodding.

"Syd," Uncle Frank said. "You're sure you're all right?"

I nodded quickly. "I am, honest." I looked back and forth between them as they exchanged a glance. "What?"

"Nothing, darling," Sunny offered up one of her smiles that lit up her whole face. "It's just… you feel delicious."

Um. Ew?

"We'll talk about it later," Uncle Frank said, though despite his assurance I was very aware of the fact he and Sunny clung to each other through a handhold turning both of their knuckles even whiter. "For now we have a job to do." He glanced across the street, eyes narrowing. "That's the place?"

Kind of hard to miss with all the wards around it. "You got it." I was suddenly feeling much more optimistic with these two in my little army.

"And your mother?" Uncle Frank met my eyes, his face schooled to expressionlessness.

"Knows about it," I said. "Hasn't acted."

His mouth tightened around the edges, but that was all he showed on the outside. "Got it."

"It's none of her business anyway," Sunny said, voice blunt. She was so matter of fact she almost made me gasp. "This is a clan issue, Syd. If there is a rogue vampire family out there, it's our job to deal with them, not the Council's."

She nodded toward the clubhouse, looking every inch the leader she became when Sebastian was gone. "This place is off campus and therefore outside your mother's purview."

Uncle Frank made a tsking sound. "That's a fine line you're walking, there, Sunshine."

She shrugged. "So the Council can bill me for the mess when I'm done. By then we'll have cleaned out this nest and moved on."

I loved Sunny for so many reasons, but mostly because she just had freaking style.

This was serious business. So why were the two of us grinning like we were having fun?

Sunny and Uncle Frank left us, staying in the shadows, approaching the house. I waited for them, mostly because I knew Sunny was right. This was their mess to clean up if the vampires inside were feeding on humans. I was just here as *their* backup.

Huh. How weird was that?

It wasn't long before the pair returned, still frowning.

"Something isn't right." Sunny chewed her lower lip a moment, staring at the house. "They are vampire wards, yes, but I'm not getting any family affiliation from them. No touch of their blood clan."

"Neither am I." Uncle Frank watched Sunny and

I realized then, no matter how much the pair of them acted like equals, she was the boss. Somehow it made me want to laugh.

She met my eyes at last. "We can break in and see what we're up against by a frontal assault," she said, "or we can wait and run more surveillance. I can bring more of our clan in if we need to, but Sebastian wants to keep this quiet and clean."

"I'm with him," I said. "Not like we need the whole city of Boston aware of what we're up to."

She nodded. "So what do you want us to do?"

Huh? Hadn't she just finished telling me this was her parade?

"Why are you asking me?"

Sunny laughed, low and deep, before kissing my cheek. "Because, coven leader," she said, "we're here for you. Whatever that means."

I looked around at the others, all staring at me like I was in charge. Which I guess I really was after all.

"We wait," I said at last, hating to, but knowing I had to have absolute proof the vampires were feeding. Not for my protection, but because I'd brought Sunny and Uncle Frank, and Sebastian and his whole blood clan by association, into this with me.

No way was I giving anyone a reason to go after them.

"Very well." Sunny squeezed my hand. "I need to see one of your friends to be sure if they are chalices."

"Sorry?" Liam's voice was soft in the darkness. "What?"

Sunny smiled at him. "Hello, Liam," she said. "Forgive me. We call humans who feed vampires willingly chalices."

"And unwillingly?" His hazel eyes were dark in the dim light.

"Dead," she said.

Clear as a bell.

"I do find it odd that witches and vampires are nesting together," Sunny said. "Your family aside, this is the first real instance of the two existing in the same place."

"There's something weird about them," I agreed. "Whatever their association, it's changing both sides. But it feels different than what's up with me. And even from Mom's power."

"Maybe because Miriam's was taken by force?" Uncle Frank slipped one arm around Sunny. "What if, like the feeding, the power exchange is done willingly?"

Sunny's face settled into a troubled frown. "I have to talk to Sebastian," she said. "We need to understand this."

"Okay," I said. "We'll all meet tomorrow night. We'll find a way to intercept Simon and Rupe so the two of you can have a look at them. Then, if they are these chalices, you and Uncle Frank can let Sebastian know. And bring in the vampire army if necessary."

Sunny's frown eased a little. "An excellent plan," she said. "We'll return to you the moment the sun sets."

I hugged them both again. "I didn't go looking for this," I said, feeling suddenly like the perpetual bearer of bad news. "I swear."

Sunny frowned again, fingers stroking my cheek. "Of course you didn't," she said. "Who said you did?"

I didn't say anything, not even when she leaned close and kissed me gently on my forehead.

"Without you, we wouldn't know any of this was happening," she said. "We're very lucky you were here paying attention."

As the vampires flickered into shadow and vanished, I couldn't help but feel better.

Take that, Quaid.

Jerktard.

32

Charlotte insisted on standing guard outside my door while Sassafras, Liam and I talked over what happened and tried to make plans. Hard to do, really, without having all the answers we needed. And really, my best plans usually involved just jumping in with all the fire power I could muster and hoping for the best.

Sassafras finally left us to go see Mom. We decided he was the best choice.

"Though I doubt she'll listen to me, either," he said. "But I'll try."

I felt a momentary pang of guilt over Meira. I'd promised I'd go visit her that night, but with everything that was happening I just couldn't. I sat on the edge of my bed, letting out a big gust of air and a gentle caress to my sister's mind.

Sorry, Meems. I have to bail on you.

It's okay. I could feel others with her, hear giggling. Sassy hadn't been kidding. Was my little sister turning into some kind of party maven? And on a school night?

Her laugh tinkled in my head as she caught my shock. *Night, Mom.* Another giggle.

Smart ass sister. Guess she wasn't missing me after all.

I let her go and turned to Liam who perched beside me, not touching me, but close enough I felt the warmth of his body. It was a great comfort to have him there, especially since Sashenka was out. I really didn't feel like being alone right then.

Until I remembered he'd kissed me and it all went awkward.

But I didn't have time to admit it. Voices on the other side of my door told me someone argued with Charlotte and when the door itself banged open and Quaid stomped in, I shot to my feet, my own anger matching the look on his face.

But he wasn't staring at me. His brown eyes were laser-focused on Liam who, to my shock, shot up and forward until he was right in Quaid's face.

Between us.

Protecting me again.

"You're not welcome here." Liam's normally kind, warm voice was full of venom. "Not after the way you treated Syd."

"Mind your own damned business, fairy boy." Quaid

shoved Liam aside. Or tried to. My tall Sidhe friend might not have had the musculature of the slightly stockier Quaid, but he did have access to enough earth magic to keep him solidly grounded, an immovable blonde wall of protectiveness.

As much as I appreciated the fact he was there for me, I didn't need the two of them fighting it out in my room like a pair of three year olds in a sandbox.

"Liam." I pulled him back, to my side while Quaid glared. "It's okay." I faced my boyfriend—or was he anymore?—down. "What are you doing here?" I kept my tone level, reasonable. "You didn't want to get involved in the trouble I'm chasing, remember?" Okay, a little dig wasn't beyond me.

Quaid's gaze shifted to me at last. "I wanted to check on you," he said. "To make sure you were okay."

"Of course she's okay," Liam grated. "Like you give a crap about her."

Quaid's brow dropped, smoldering fire burning in his eyes as his magic coiled around him, hands clenching into fists. "This is a private conversation," he rumbled in his deep voice, "in case you hadn't noticed."

"Boys!" I sighed, caught Charlotte's arched eyebrows and apologetic expression before I physically put myself between them, the buzz of Liam's earth magic humming on one side while Quaid's thrummed like a taut drum on the other. "Enough. Quaid, Liam was here to help me. No offense, but you weren't." I felt myself sag a little. "I guess I understand why you said no. But I had to do something, with or without you." Sadness finally won over the anger I'd cultivated. I didn't want it to go like this, none of it, not the hurt look on Liam's face as he realized I'd approached Quaid first and not the deep pain in Quaid's when he decided I'd replaced him.

Damn them both.

"I should have been there for you," Quaid said, whole layers of meaning behind his words. "I'm sorry, Syd."

I shook my head. "Just forget it," I said. "I have more important things to worry about."

He flinched a little, eyes going to Liam's face. "I'm happy to help," he said between clenched teeth. "And so are all of my friends. But you can't have it both ways, Syd." His dark eyes, almost black from the intensity of his feelings, locked on me and made my stomach do a slow roll. "You have to choose."

Choose? What was he talking about?

I finally understood when Liam laughed, a harsh and angry sound. "You're an asshole, Quaid. Always have been, always will be."

Wait a second. Choose between them? He so did not just ask me to—

"That's not fair." I turned my back fully on Liam to face Quaid. "Liam's my friend. He's here for me when I need him. When you're off with your Enforcer friends, with... with her." We both knew who I was talking about. "He's been there for me when you weren't. If I have to give up Liam, you have to give up your friends too."

Quaid shook his head, backing away. "You just don't get it," he said. "You don't see it. Not like I do."

Fury rose again, smothering the grief. Good. I liked the anger much better.

"Liam's right," I said. "You are an asshole. Get out of my room."

His face went cold, still. "Fine," he said, "have your little fling. I'm done. So much for love, Syd."

Quaid stormed off, leaving me there with my heart torn open. I felt Liam reach for me, but couldn't, just couldn't and ran from the room, after the love of my life.

I caught him in the Yard, feet from his own dorm, nabbed his arm, spun him around. Quaid's own rage was clear on his face, even as he grabbed me and pulled me against his chest, lips coming down hard on mine. I let him kiss me, despite the pain, until his anger was too much, overwhelming me, making my demon furious.

When I jerked free of him, she took control of my body for a split second and slapped him so hard he staggered.

As he straightened, my whole body went cold, chilled to the bone, goosebumps standing on my arms. Quaid's face was so forlorn, his own hurt so clear I wanted to reach for him, but didn't.

Didn't.

He slumped, moisture standing in his beautiful eyes, his power gently touching mine. "Syd," he whispered. "What's happening to us?"

"We're just screwed up, I guess." I hugged myself, wishing it was his arms around me. "Who is she to you, Quaid? And why aren't you with me?"

"You're making me crazy." His hands jammed into the back pockets of his jeans. "I love you so much I can hardly breathe sometimes. I can't think. I don't know what to do, Syd."

"But." It was there. It had always been there, that but.

"I love the Enforcers." He met my eyes, his emotions under control. "I want to be one."

"You know you can't have both." Now I sounded like him. But it was true and we both understood it. The law said Enforcers couldn't have family affiliations. Had to remain objective and were only allowed to tie in to the Council magic.

Which meant no marriage. No life together.

Nothing.

Could I live with that? Worse, could I live with a Quaid who gave up what he wanted for my happiness?

I couldn't leave it alone. "Who is she to you, Quaid?"

"Payten is just a friend." He shrugged. But I read the guilt in him. Maybe at this point they were still just friends. But he knew what she wanted. And he wasn't fighting it very hard.

"Liam is my friend too," I said. Did he read into that what I read into his words? Perhaps.

Quaid bobbed a nod.

"You have to choose," I said. "We can't do this anymore. You know that, right?" I reached out, touched his arm. "We've spent the last two years locked in this thing together, Quaid. But it's not good for either of us if it's going to keep on going this way. You hurting me. Me hurting you back."

Though he was the one doing most of the hurting, I didn't press the issue.

"I'll choose when you do," he said.

Of all the stubborn, arrogant, jealous… I let my anger out again, not caring how much damage I did.

"I chose you long ago, you idiot," I said. "You're the only one who can't seem to accept that."

I didn't give him a chance to answer, turning away from him, not able to stand being around him any longer.

How was it fair nobody warned me how much love sucked?

Liam was gone by the time I returned to my room, Charlotte remaining a respectful distance behind me. Nice of her. Either that or she just wanted to avoid my temper.

I stood there in my dorm, brain running in a circle before I turned and left again. This was ridiculous. I had to sort it out and the only way to do that was to talk to Liam.

We were friends. The kiss was just a mistake, a slip up. I'd hash it out with my Sidhe friend and then go shove it in Quaid's face.

Part of me ached with sympathy for Quaid. He'd never known real love, not as a child, a toy and a power source in the hands of the Moromonds, then a spy among the Dumonts searching for the means to avenge his parent's deaths. The only time he'd ever come in contact with people who really cared about him was in my family, and those moments were brief. I knew he was a good person, deep down. He'd proven it to me over and over again, between bouts of jerkishness. But was the damage done too profound for him to move past?

Even if we worked things out this time, would we ever really find peace together?

I refused to accept the answer might be no.

The moment I spotted Liam's slumped form on a bench at the edge of the Yard, I felt a pang of nerves. But I shoved them aside. This was too important for me to wimp out. We'd talk about it, laugh over the silliness of what happened and everything would be okay again.

I sat next to him, reaching for his hand which he took instantly.

"I'm sorry about the fight," he said. "It was stupid."

I leaned in, resting my head on his shoulder. "It *was* stupid," I said. "You two idiots. I could have knocked your heads together."

He grunted softly, a small smile on his face. "Yeah," he said.

"But Quaid's the worst." I sat up, shaking my head. "Thinking he has something to be jealous about. I don't know what I'm going to do with him. He's such a freak."

I glanced at Liam, only had a second to process he was closer to me until his lips touched mine, a soft, gentle touch so different from the rough one I'd just shared with Quaid my heart fluttered in my chest.

When Liam pulled away, his hazel eyes were wide open,

his heart in them. "He has a lot to be jealous about," Liam said. "I've been in love with you since the moment we met."

I should have felt more surprised. Hadn't I just convinced myself this was nothing, that Quaid was full of it? That Liam was just my friend.

In my heart, I'd known. So what did that say about me?

Liam went on while I struggled with my conscience. "I never said anything, did anything, because I knew how much you love Quaid." Liam's free hand clenched into a fist, but the one holding mine was as gentle as ever. As gentle as he was. "But I can't stand it, Syd. Seeing how he treats you. You deserve so much better—to be loved and adored and made the center of his universe." Liam sat back, shoulders tense, whole body rigid. "I'm sorry. I can't hide how I feel about you anymore. But I'll understand if you choose Quaid." Liam's gaze dropped. "I just want to be around you, no matter what that means, even if we can't be together. Even if you never love me the way I love you."

He might as well have ripped my heart out of my chest, tossed it to the ground at his feet and danced a jig on it. Sobs built inside me, but I couldn't let them out, just sat there, numb and unable to react to anything he said. When I finally could move it was to rise and leave him there, half running from the sweet, kind and amazing guy I adored.

But didn't love. Not like that.

Please, please, I didn't want to lose him over this.

I reached instinctively for Quaid, wanting to feel him, to have his power wrap me up, to embrace the familiar touch of his magic. But the moment I did he muted our connection, cutting me off from him, from his love and from his magic.

My demon howled her fury and slashed out with amber fire, cutting the tie between us in her grief. I instantly shoved her back, but it was too late.

The damage was done.

The line of love I'd clung to so many times, the piece of Quaid I'd held close to me and used for comfort for so long was gone. Cut free. I sent my magic to him, begging to reconnect.

For whatever reason, Quaid refused to let me back in.

The sobs building inside me from Liam's confession rose higher, threatening to choke me, to shatter me into so many pieces I was certain I'd never be able to put them back together again.

Only one thought crossed my mind. And with my heart shattering over and over again, my soul dying, I ran across the Yard, just wanting my mother.

34

Of course Maurice didn't want to let me in, but I was in no shape to listen, to pay attention. My demon, still raging and hurting, shoved him aside as I forced my way into Mom's quarters, calling for her in mind and voice.

I just really needed my mother to hug me and let me cry and tell me everything was going to be all right. Because if she did, if that happened, I knew everything would be.

Not how things turned out.

Mom stormed out of her office, her fury apparent, power slamming into me and bringing me to a rocking halt. "Sydlynn Thaddea Hayle!" She blocked off my attempt to reach her with my mind, the slap of her power so harsh it broke through my desperate grief and made everything clear again. "You cannot just barge in here and demand attention any time you want it!"

I gaped at her, her anger the final blow my heart could take.

"You're not a little girl anymore," Mom said. "If you have a problem, deal with it."

Everything I was feeling suddenly shattered outward, shards of my emotions making it past her shields, cutting through until she winced. Stopped. Flushed and paled. Reached out one hand to me.

"Syd," she whispered. "I'm sorry."

Too late. Far too late for that.

"I'm sorry to have disturbed you, Council Leader," I managed to mumble as I staggered backward, toward the door, not wanting her to touch me or look at me, blocking off her power and the sympathy she tried to share, fighting my way back out of the room to gasp for air while I waited for the elevator.

"Syd." Erica was there, arms trying to encircle me, but I fought her off, shoved her back.

"Stop." I didn't mean to be cruel. But she wasn't my mother. Neither was Mom. Not anymore.

The elevator doors closed on me just as Meira raced toward them, calling my name.

No.

This couldn't be happening. I needed to focus. I had a job to do, friends to save. I would not let Quaid destroy me, would not allow my friendship with Liam to tear a giant hole in my soul.

I collapsed against one of the big trees and sobbed silently into the darkness, hands pressed to my face to keep sound from escaping. Charlotte hovered somewhere nearby, but I was grateful she didn't come closer.

I'm here, girl. And Gram's power wrapped around me, pulled me close and she drew me to her so I could let out all of my pain into her. The part of her that lived in me for so long returned for a moment, filling me up with so much love I cried harder when she pulled away. But they were cleansing tears now, not the empty, tearing sobs trying to destroy me.

Gram. I smeared the tears away with the heels of my hands. *How did everything get so messed up?*

It's love, she sent, gruff but kind. *Nothing ever goes as planned.*

She'd know. Her husband betrayed her and the whole coven, a traitor planted by Odette and Naudia Dumont.

My heart went out to her, then, to my amazing grandmother. *You're here for me,* I sent. *But was anyone ever there for you?*

Doesn't matter now, she answered. *Are you all right?*

I drew a shaking breath, did a quick, silent exam of myself. *Yes. I am.* And I was. Mostly. The hurt was still there, but I could live with it.

Best you can hope for. Gram's power held me another moment. *I'm always here. Remember that.*

She let me go even as I hugged the feeling of her to me and wished I could go home and hold her for real.

I almost acted, reaching for the veil, when Sassafras's mental voice broke through what was left of my grief.

The Dumont brothers are on the move.

So? I didn't mean to be short with him, but I wasn't exactly a hundred percent.

So, he shot back, *they have company.*

The image of Rupe and Simon walking side-by-side with Jean Marc and Kristophe was enough to shove all of my crap down and send me running.

What were the Dumont brothers doing with my friends? I kicked myself as I considered the possibilities—and failed to realize I should have been watching the clubhouse for them to leave as well as enter. We could have had the pair of them instead of now chasing them for the second time that night, this time in worse company.

At least in my opinion.

I was so grateful for the chance to focus on a disaster I eagerly dove into the veil, almost forgetting Charlotte who lunged to grip my hand at the last second. Kudos to her for not saying anything, and not judging me even for a second. I could tell from the calm and steady look on her face when we emerged onto Holyoke nothing had changed for her.

Naturally I arrived the moment Rupe and Simon passed through the door, Jean Marc and Kristophe right behind them. Was it just me or did they seem hesitant? Maybe Darin was widening his net to include witches he deemed worthy.

Which said nothing for his taste.

I was about to turn to Sassafras who sat at my feet, growling softly, when a long, black car pulled up to the front of the Star Club and the back passenger door opened.

My stomach clenched as my eyes traveled over the black-cloaked figure, the set of her shoulders—yes, it was a she— the way she carried her head even inside her hood. I knew her, knew her in the pit of my gut, in the burning fury in my veins, absolutely, without a doubt.

Didn't need the confirmation of her identity when Ameline Benoit turned her head, her profile clear in the light of a street lamp before she swept her way up the steps to the front door and let herself inside.

My entire body shook with the need to go after her, to pound her into the ground with the power of my magic, to turn her into a wet lump of flesh and blood and splintered bone I would then happily dance through while I cackled my madness.

Ameline.

Gram was rubbing off on me.

"How?" Charlotte's shock made her look years younger. "I don't smell her." She turned to me as if this was my fault. "How, Syd?"

I shook my head, letting my anger simmer. I'd need it

later. Yes, I would. "I have no idea," I said. "But we're not going to wait until tomorrow night to find out."

Sassafras growled softly. "Now we have to act," he said. "If only to take her into custody."

"She tried to kill me," I said, "and is wanted by the Council. Which gives me every right to break those wards and go after her." My demon hummed her happiness, her eagerness to kill while Shaylee shivered in the imagined pleasure of ripping Ameline's black heart out and feeding it to her.

Only the vampire inside me was still. Enough of an anchor I had the presence of mind to reach out to Uncle Frank and Sunny.

Ameline's here, I told them. *We're moving now.*

They arrived in a shudder of shadow only a moment later. "You're certain it was her?"

Charlotte was still struggling with the truth, muttering to herself in her native language, guttural and angry.

"I'm positive," I said. I turned to the weregirl and grasped her arm, shaking her a little. Charlotte looked up, met my gaze, rage showing in her face.

"That bitch," she said. "How did she hide from me?"

"I need you to go to Mom," I said. "Charlotte, you have to tell her what's going on." No way was I reaching for my mother. She could get the news second hand, after I'd torn Ameline and the brothers Dumont brand new gaping holes where none had been before. "Do you understand?"

But Charlotte jerked free of me, shaking her head, her wolf in her eyes, twisting the skin of her face.

"Never," she snarled. "I will not leave you. Nor will you take from me the chance to have vengeance."

"I'll go." Sassafras stood up, shaking himself. "Now that we know Ameline is here, Miriam will have to listen." He scampered off into the darkness before I could stop him, not that I would have. He was right. If Mom would finally pay attention and act, it would be under Sassy's scathing demands.

"No more sneaking," Sunny said. "We're going in the front door, no surprises."

"Agreed," I said. "I'm tired of standing around."

As I turned toward the Star Club, I felt Liam's mind reach for mine. The tentativeness giving way to worry, then a surge of protectiveness as he felt what I was doing.

I'm on my way.

He might have been, but I wasn't waiting.

I drew in my power, letting it build and build, a delicious, horrible joy filling me up at the act. This was the feeling, the stirring of greatness, what it meant to be powerful.

I embraced my magic, the flood of demon fire, the surge of Sidhe energy. It didn't matter to me the vampire held her peace. I pulled in the family magic at last, felt Gram stir and back me up, the entire coven coming to my call as I faced the door to the club and smashed down the wards with a single blast of my power.

The door flew inward, splintering around the edges, the shields collapsing with an almost audible sigh until the entire place was defenseless. Sunny and Uncle Frank flashed forward, up the steps and inside while I strode in, Charlotte beside me, like I owned the place.

"Honey," I called as I stepped over the remains of the door, "I'm home."

Empty. Sunny flickered into the wide hallway I found myself in from a nearby entry and shook her head. No way the place was empty.

No way.

I checked every room myself, felt around with my power. Stood in the middle of the main room at the end of the hall and fumed as I spun in a slow circle and realized we'd been led on a wild goose chase.

No one. The place was silent.

Liam panted his way down the hall, coming to a gasping halt just inside the door to the fine parlor with its stupid leather seats and velvet curtains and crystal studded chandeliers. I wanted to puke, to scream, to tear the place down with my bare hands.

Where were they?

"Syd." Charlotte stood near the back of the room, sniffing at one of the curtains. "Here."

I was at her side, the two vampires with me, Liam hovering behind, as Charlotte jerked the curtain wide. Exposing a door.

Cowards. They were hiding from me.

She was reaching for it just as I felt the pressure of a ward breaking, like a bubble being popped, outward toward us. I had only a moment to grab her by the back of her jacket and jerk her away before the door burst open and a rush of bodies came through.

I fought without thinking, sending the attackers flying, spinning, bodies crumpling into walls and furniture, not realizing until we'd almost subdued all of them who I was bringing down. Students, normal students, some of whom I recognized just in passing from seeing them on campus, at least twenty or more of them, practically frothing at the mouth, eyes crazed, skin pale.

Thralled. Chalices. Both.

Witch and vampire magic together.

Abomination, the vampire inside me whispered.

I spun on Uncle Frank and Liam who mopped up the last of the first line of defense. "You two stay up here and contain this mess then search the rest of the house." I gestured then to Sunny. "The three of us have a job to do."

I didn't give the boys a chance to argue, heading for the dark stairs while my bodywere crept down them, her shape altering as she went, the low hum of her wolf's voice making my bones vibrate, the steady power of Sunny pressing close behind me.

I just barely reached the bottom step, eyes searching the artificial darkness, even my demon vision unable to penetrate it when light flared, blinding me a moment and making both Sunny and Charlotte cry out as their photosensitive eyes were assaulted.

I blinked through the tears of returning vision, power wrapped tightly around me, knowing we could be attacked at any second, not surprised when I was finally able to see, the first face that swam into my vision was Ameline's.

"Hello, Syd," she said. "I'm so glad you could make it."

36

The dark basement, stone walls weeping with moisture, was full of more bodies, though most of these had their own wits about them. Charlotte hissed, crouching as the wolf inside her reacted to the dozen or so vampires who lurked around the edges of the large space, though the leader, the vamp I recognized from the attack on me in the Yard and from just earlier that night as he escorted my friends into the house the first time, stood next to Ameline on her left as though they were friends. If the evil-to-the-core witch had friends. Most likely she was simply using him and would discard him when it was convenient for her.

Or whenever he became inconvenient.

About another dozen witches, all young, hovered behind Darin who stood at Ameline's right hand. The smile on his face, so twisted he lost all semblance of humanity, made me want to shove it through the back of his head.

Couldn't wait, actually.

Only two thralled subjects remained amid all the magic

users and creatures in that basement—my friends, Rupe and Simon. Rupe sat at Ameline's feet, one of her hands locked in his hair, though from the way he leaned into her touch it was clear he liked it.

Ew.

Simon on the other hand knelt in front of Darin and looked more out of it than aware. The sight of him crushed and broken in the hands of my enemies was almost enough to start the fight. Almost. If it weren't for Sunny's steady presence and the ever-soft calm of the vampire inside me, I'm sure I would have acted before I had all the facts. The last time I'd underestimated Ameline I'd almost died in the parking lot at the Hilltop Hotel in Wilding Springs. This time I didn't have Mia to bail me out.

"Welcome to the Star Club." Darin's giggle came out girly, but he didn't seem to care, obviously just excited I was here. Which meant, of course, he thought they'd won.

I couldn't bring myself to be afraid.

It didn't help his case when Ameline casually turned and struck him. The blow seemed inconsequential, but the witch staggered and fell to his hands and knees next to Simon, blood gushing from his broken nose.

"Your place, little witch," Ameline said in her crystal

clear voice, flat and emotionless as her piercing blue eyes stared into me. "Remember it."

He groveled at her feet, but couldn't reach her because Simon was in the way. Rupe. "Forgive me, mistress."

I allowed my power out to check the rest of the house while she entertained herself. And came across sleeping witches, all older. All adults, even as Uncle Frank and Liam paused to check on each of them. "What have you done to the others?"

"Nothing," Ameline said. "Except silence those who don't clearly see my vision."

So they were more than sleeping. I felt that now, their life-forces waning. Had the vampires fed on them? There wasn't much I could do about it at the moment, not until I'd crushed the stunningly evil girl into the cold stone floor.

Ameline's lips quirked slightly as she went back to running her fingers through Rupe's hair. "I saw this delicious one with Mia," she said. "And simply had to have him." Blue eyes glittered. "I take it you don't approve."

I shrugged. "Not like you to bother with normals."

She laughed softly, the sound making my skin crawl though most people would have found it charming. "He'll do for now," she said. "And will make a lovely meal later."

Rupe smiled up at her in absolute adoration while I found my stomach curling.

"Meal?" She was going to eat him? Had she become some kind of cannibal? I knew she was a blood magic user, but what was that doing to her?

Too late, lost in my confusion, I noticed the vampires oozed forward and now had us cut off, Sunny's back to me, Charlotte's too so we formed a little protective triangle of power. I raised my shields around them, lending them my strength if they needed it, but knew they could take care of themselves.

"Piotr," Sunny said. "What is the meaning of this?"

The lead vampire smiled at her. Wait, she knew him?

"Dear Teresa," he said, dark eyes matching his long black hair and floor-length leather coat. "It's been too long. Your family has missed you, my dear."

Now, I was pretty sure my whole life Sunny wasn't Sunny's real name. But I'd never asked her real one, partly out of respect for the past I knew she regretted. Hearing her real name thrown out there with such casual disdain sent my temper flaring higher.

But Sunny had it handled. "You are no longer my family," she said. "I'm a DeWinter now."

"So you claim," Piotr drifted closer, his vampires

tightening around us while Ameline smiled and watched. "But your blood calls to blood, Teresa, and you cannot resist those who made you." What was that accent? Something European. Not French, more guttural, but not as harsh as Charlotte's.

"The vampire who turned me is dead," she said.

"But the blood line he came from isn't." Piotr reached out to touch her cheek, but couldn't through the hum of my shield. "And we own you, as much as we ever have."

"The Blood Clan Wilhelm has no hold over me," she said. "See for yourself."

He frowned at her, suddenly not so cocky. Sunny turned her head, whispered to me. "Just trust me," she said. "Let him in."

Eep. She was asking a lot. But I parted the way, because it was Sunny and she'd never let me down when it really counted.

Piotr touched her cheek then, his long fingers stroking over the flawless flesh. White fire burned in Sunny's eyes as he tried to wrap her up in his power. There was a brief flare of light I squinted away from, only to find his power falling away from her even as Sunny laughed.

"What have you done?" Piotr's frown was more shocked than upset.

"I told you," she said. "I'm a DeWinter now. My leader, Sebastian, drained me, my clan filling me back up again."

That sounded... dangerous. From the horror on Piotr's face, I was right.

"It should have killed you." He pulled away from her, his vampires falling back as though they were affected by his disbelief.

"My family sustained me," she said, pride shining in her, power rolling forward as she shoved him back. "Something my birth clan never did." Her smile was as bright as the sun she was named for as she shuddered softly, blonde hair rippling. I'd never seen her so beautiful. "I'm free of your evil forever," she said.

Piotr retreated, his vampires moving away with him. The small smile on Ameline's face was now gone as her forehead pinched in the barest of frowns and when she spoke her voice was as icy cold as her heart.

"Kill her," she said. "I brought you here for a reason."

So Ameline knew I'd recruit Sunny to help. Of course. Way to start a vampire war, you bitch.

But Piotr shook his head, his long black hair shuddering with the motion. "I have no jurisdiction," he said. "She's not a Wilhelm any longer."

"So what?" Ameline pointed at Sunny, her fury finally showing. "Kill her!"

"I was more than willing to remove her from DeWinter's grasp," Piotr grated at her, "but that was when I thought she was still one of us." His dark eyes drifted over Sunny again, in a way that made me wonder if they had a real history. A personal history. "But I have no claim over her. And if I were to attack her now, it would mean instigating a war between clans. That I am not authorized to do."

"You've broken lots of rules so far." Ameline was practically spitting in rage.

He drew himself up, as cold as she had been, pulling away from her like he only then understood with whom he had allied himself. "No," he said, "I've only tampered with mortals and witches. They are fair game. But to break clan law… that I will not do."

Ameline's hand lashed out, much as it had when she struck Darin, but Piotr was a vampire, faster, stronger. He caught her wrist in his hand and held her while he sneered down into her furious face.

"Be grateful you still have the support of my mistress," he said. "Or you would be dead for daring to strike me, witch."

Ameline jerked free of him. "Fool, weakling. Don't you

see? None of this matters." She glared at me. "None of it. It's just the first step, one small step that would have made my job easier. I don't need you anymore."

"What are you up to, Ameline?" I kept my tone light, knowing it would piss her off. "It seems like your little alliance here is falling apart. And the witches who supported you aren't exactly up to your standards."

She glared down at Darin who still groveled beside her. "Inferior," she snarled before her face schooled back to blank ice. "But they don't matter either. Not while I continue to gather those to me with the vision and foresight to use the power we were destined to wield."

Blood magic. Had to be. My heart clenched as I stopped to take a breath.

"You're creating a coven," I said as the understanding of her real purpose dawned. "A blood coven."

Ameline laughed then, harsh and grating, not her usual tinkle of pretty false joy. "Very good, Sydlynn," she said. "I see I've underestimated you again. A pity. But yes, you're correct. These," she waved at Darin and the witches who waited for her orders, "are my first members. But I have more, don't you see?" Madness tinted her eyes red as the blood magic she'd been using rose to the surface. "Many more, everywhere. The movement is growing. Soon I will be strong enough to take on the Council."

"And after them?" I wanted to brush off the whole world domination thing, but she was just scary enough in that moment I really believed she would do it.

Ameline shrugged. "Things are about to change," she said.

I had to stop her. And now that her vampire supporters seemed to be backing down, we had a better chance of doing so. Hopefully.

But attacking Ameline took a back seat when the door at the top of the basement stairs slammed open and Mia leaped down them, her magic propelling her forward while she shrieked like a woman possessed.

Right. At. Ameline.

37

I thought she might do it, succeed at killing Ameline, save me the trouble, but the moment Mia came close to her hated rival, red energy flared. My friend impacted the barrier, her lavender family magic zinging against the blood power, throwing her back toward me.

Toward us.

Sunny caught her, eased her to the ground, a little stunned, but unharmed. I was certain if she wasn't a coven leader, if she didn't have all the family magic at her disposal, Mia would be charcoal. Instead she staggered to her feet, eyes blazing with insanity.

"Give him BACK!"

For a moment I couldn't believe what I'd heard. Him? Ameline was about to try to take over the world and Mia was focused on Rupe? Until I understood her state, the importance she'd placed on him, on the guy she knew as Blood, probably the first person she'd ever met who loved her and didn't judge her or try to make her be someone she wasn't. To Mia, Rupe was a lifeline, her reason for being.

Which meant we were in big trouble. Because from the look on his face, the way he rejected Mia with everything about him, told me as weak as she was, she was about to be crushed.

"I'm with the woman of my dreams," Rupe said. "Strong, beautiful." He looked up at Ameline with a smile and she smiled back. "Not some weak girl who doesn't know who she is." Rupe snorted, disdain clear on his face. "You really thought I could ever love you?"

Mia's face crumpled and I was reaching for her, to hold her up, when her family magic flared around her, rage consuming her face so quickly I worried she'd finally shattered her mind.

"TRAITOR!" Something flickered behind Ameline's right shoulder even as Mia dissolved into a shrieking, ineffectual mess.

I knew that flicker. Called it out with my magic until Alison was full form, floating behind my enemy.

More betrayal, then. Her eyes were still black, but from the unhappy twist to her mouth a part of the girl I knew still remained.

Ameline glanced over her shoulder at Alison before laughing at me. "Ah yes," she said. "Your little echo."

Now I knew who had been feeding Alison's jealousy, who drove her to steal the vampire essence from me. The "she" Alison talked about. And I also knew now Ameline had known exactly where I was at all times, her little spy following me everywhere.

The weight of that betrayal wasn't as heavy as it could have been. Not while I still struggled with my guilt.

Charlotte grumbled next to me. "I still can't smell her," she said. "Why can't I smell her?"

A very good question. "Yes, Ameline," I said, "why is that? It's been driving poor Charlotte here crazy not knowing. New perfume?"

Her answering smile was dry. "Simple," she said, "I'm the furthest along the hybrid path. Maybe I was right before when I assumed you were stupid, Sydlynn."

Feel her. The vampire inside me whispered, soft and subtle, but I heard her, loud and clear. And without warning, sent her toward Ameline, the vampire power penetrating the blood magic as though it didn't exist.

Well now. Wasn't that interesting? No more so than the feeling of Ameline, the coldness penetrating her expression and diving deep inside her.

Oh. My. Swearword.

"What have you done?" My words came out in a whisper as the vampire inside me finally stirred at last.

Ameline ran one hand down her own arm as if enjoying her own touch. "I've made myself perfect."

Witch, yes. And vampire. The power all wound together inside her. But she didn't have access to the essence I had. Instead, she'd stolen power from vampires and absorbed it into herself.

I could feel the energy devouring her, even as her witch magic healed her, forming a battling symbiosis, a never-ending war for her soul.

She'd mentioned making a meal of Rupe. She hadn't meant eating his flesh.

No. She just wanted to drink his blood.

"The ways of the maji are diverse and complex," Ameline hissed, white fire warring with red inside her eyes. "But they held themselves back, were creators of nothing. I am adapting myself to use what they could only fear to imagine. And this is just the beginning."

I found myself shaking my head, horrified by what she was becoming. "This will kill you," I said.

"I had wanted the virus you carry," she went on as if I hadn't spoken, "but these fools couldn't deliver."

Piotr scowled at her. "We've given you more than enough," he said.

"I've taken what I deserve," she snarled back. "And I'm not done yet."

"Piotr," Sunny said, voice quiet, "you must know now she's mad. Yvette must be warned, this evil one destroyed."

He hesitated, frown so deep it cast shadows in the creases of his face. "I shall consider it," he said.

Ameline's laugh was high-pitched. "Fools," she said. "I'm stronger than you know. And growing more so by the day. You can't stop me, not now." She glared at me. "And when I kill you, Sydlynn, I will have that vampire power you carry inside you for my own."

Never, she whispered in my head. *I will destroy myself first.*

Ameline jerked back on Rupe's hair, pulling him closer. "And when I'm done with the vampires, I'll go after the Sidhe next. Fill myself up with their magic until I am the queen of the earth itself."

"And then Demonicon, I suppose." The idea she could even consider taking on the entire demon plane was ludicrous.

Wasn't it?

Ameline settled at last, though the madness never left her. "The power of the sorcerers will be my final conquest," she said. "And then I will be unstoppable."

Piotr didn't seem as upset by her plans as I really thought he should have. And from the grim look on Sunny's face, I knew she wasn't holding her breath we might have allies in his blood clan.

"Now," Ameline said, her power surging around her as she called up the red mingled with the white, a spinning column devouring the blue she siphoned from Darin and his witches, all of whom moaned and collapsed to the floor as she drained them, "we end this."

I felt her shields reach out to block us off from the outside world. So it had been she who restored Darin's shredded protections, she who warded the house. I had to be faster than her.

We definitely needed reinforcements.

And the first mind I thought of to reach for help was Quaid's.

Though our connection was gone, I sent everything I had and it was more than enough. His momentary anger at me slamming into his mind vanished when I threw the picture of what I faced into his head and just as Ameline's wards sealed up and cut me off, I felt him running.

Toward me.

Cavalry called. Now all we had to do was survive until they arrived. Though I suddenly had doubts about any of our survival as Ameline spun and pointed at two young witches. Witches who died in a flood of blood from their torn out throats as two of the vampires showed their true loyalty and released the precious liquid she needed to feed her power.

I knew there was nothing I could do against so much blood magic, but no way was I giving up, not now, not ever.

My Sidhe power held her back as Ameline drew in the rush of magic suddenly available to her, flooding the basement with a mist of red stinging my eyes and skin and making my lungs ache. Shaylee cried out, tried to flee from the touch of the cloud as we all, my demon and Sidhe princess and I, realized what it was at the same moment— not just magic, but blood itself, infused with power and suspended and feeding Ameline with every single pinprick of it when it touched exposed skin or reached our lungs.

Which meant it was attacking everyone in the room. Yes, even the vampires themselves, Ameline's so-called allies now crumpling with horrible cries, their skin seeming to weep red where the mist touched them. Piotr collapsed to the damp stone, one hand reaching for Sunny.

She, at least, wasn't down for the count yet, thanks to my

shielding, but I was weakening too fast, more and more of the mist reaching us, and I knew she only had seconds.

The door crashed open again, Uncle Frank and Liam storming their way downstairs. Liam's Sidhe power bubbled outward, covering him and the two vampires as Sunny fell to her knees, both hands clutching her damaged face. He was just foreign enough, I could only guess, Ameline without access yet to Sidhe power, that Liam was able to hold off the mist while Uncle Frank sheltered Sunny. But I could also see the strain on his face and knew his barrier of protection was stretched to its limit.

Which meant Charlotte, Mia and I were on our own. Not that I expected much help from the damaged leader of the Dumont coven, not while she sat on the floor, sobbing and muttering to herself.

Shaylee's power finally collapsed, her magic tied too closely to mine, making her vulnerable, leaving bigger gaps in my shields, gaps my demon struggled to fill, her amber power burning away some of the mist. It wasn't until she howled her fury I felt not only the burn and sting of the mist, but the pull of it as well.

Ameline was feeding on me.

The bitch.

And there was nothing I could do to stop her. Not while

my demon whimpered and did her best, my witch magic spiraling around me, the family power writhing in its own agony as Ameline pulled more and more free, feeding not only herself, but the very cloud of blood until I could barely see through it, just enough I knew she stood above me now, the outline of her vague, but her burning eyes gazing down on me as though she owned me.

"And now, Sydlynn Hayle," she said in a voice that vibrated with so much power I knew I was done for, "I shall take what is mine, both the Dumont family magic and your own Hayle power, and you and the life forces inside you will feed me, grant me their unique magics, until you die."

She crouched next to me, fingers running through the cloud of blood, clearing a path through it so I could see her, smearing it over her lips, licking her fingers until her mouth dripped crimson.

Weak, unable to counter her, feeling Gram beating against the connection between us, blocked off by the power of Ameline's blood magic, I refused to quit even though the world began to darken around the edges as unconsciousness threatened.

Until the vampire inside me roared to life with a surge of power. *ENOUGH!*

Ameline must have seen or felt the essence of the vampire wake inside me because the draw on my power ended abruptly as her eyes flew very wide, mouth hanging open.

I have to admit I was more than a little shocked myself to find myself standing suddenly over her, even more that I didn't have anything to do with the movements of my body. I'd had my demon take me over before, but this was different.

Very, very different.

"Listen to me, witch child," the vampire said, reaching out with my hand to touch Ameline's forehead. The moment she did, the mist collapsed, pattering to the floor in a rain of blood, soaking everything. But at least I could breathe.

Ameline rocked back on her heels, face slack as the vampire went on.

"What you are creating, what you seek and desire, can never be. The maji knew it. I was formed in an effort to do what you are attempting. They failed. The greatest powers of their kind failed." She lashed out with white magic, knocking Ameline on her butt in the blood with a wet smack. "What makes you think you can do better?"

Ameline scrambled to her feet, a great effort on the slippery floor. But the vampire let her rise, watched her with a mix of anger and cold detachment, while I struggled to regain the power stolen from me.

But Ameline was still powerful, beyond me, and I could do nothing about it.

The vampire could.

I felt it, the draw of magic returning to me, the familiar feel I remembered from the night Ameline and the Dumont brothers attacked me, when the vampire essence stole her power and almost crippled her. This time the pull was much more powerful. Free of her prison, the vampire inside me had free rein. And she didn't hesitate to return what belonged to me.

Ameline wailed, back pedaled, her hands flapping in front of her as though that could sever the touch of the vampire. But she didn't need to touch my enemy, the initial contact was more than enough. I could almost see a huge rope stretching between us, like a power cable, feeding back from Ameline and into me.

Into us. Shaylee surged to full power, my demon roaring her joy and defiance while the vampire's displeasure drove

Ameline back and back until she stood among the ruin of her new coven.

But the vampire wasn't done. She sent all the power out of Ameline, back into those she'd stolen from. The undead ones Ameline recruited quickly recovered, as did Darin and his witches, now shaking their heads and looking around as though she'd held them thrall.

Which she probably had. Even Simon slumped, head falling forward as if he'd been released.

Only then did I notice Jean Marc and Kristophe cowering in the corner, hidden all this time by vampires and other witches. They the vampire essence left empty.

Instead, she funneled their power to me. I resisted at first, the taint of their lavender magic almost too much. But once it reached me it purified, melding with the Hayle family magic until it was clean again.

"Your evil will not be allowed to continue." The vampire wasn't done. Ameline was now stripped again, to her core, but the vampire didn't stop. I watched the girl's face begin to whither and age, her hands shrinking and becoming lined and hollow. Ameline screamed as she touched her face, eyes full of terror and the most hate I'd ever seen.

I reached out to join the vampire in containing her. This had to end. But before I could complete the ward around her, Ameline spun, jerking a knife from her pocket, driving the blade into Darin's neck.

Fresh blood magic surged outward, so powerful even the vampire essence was knocked backward. Ameline's features were restored in a flash, but the hate remained as she shuddered and vanished in a cloud of red fire.

"My love!" Rupe's wail drove a blade of its own through me. "Don't leave me!"

There was no protecting him when the red power appeared again and carried him off.

"No!" Mia was finally aware, it seemed, falling forward, one hand in the blood, the other reaching for the vanished Rupe. She then collapsed, passed out, eyelids fluttering and I knew she'd never be the same.

The house upstairs was suddenly alive with thudding footsteps, shouting, witch magic. Distracted, I glanced away and back again, seeing Liam slump as he released the shield, catching one last flicker from a basement full of frightened witches and vampires.

To see Alison staring at her hands. Covered in blood. Lift them to her mouth.

Taste it.

Meet my gaze with her blacked out eyes. And laugh as her body flooded with life.

Only to disappear.

Oh crap.

That can't be good. I spoke directly to the essence. She sighed, sinking back inside me and returning to her quiet, calm state.

No, she agreed. *Though now I know I have chosen well, Sydlynn Hayle. In you.*

There was that, at least.

A wall of Enforcers pounded their way down toward us, Quaid among them. He met my eyes, his full of fear for me. I raised my weary hand and saluted him.

"Still think I went looking for trouble?"

40

Mom's face told me everything I needed to know. Sure, she'd been all official and supportive when the Enforcers were around, when the Council demanded an emergency meeting and we were presented as heroes, my friends and I. But now, hours later, in the wee dawn of an approaching new day with no one around to see it, she didn't look happy.

Nope. Not happy at all.

"What were you thinking?" She faced down Uncle Frank first, shaking she was so furious.

"We did what we had to do," he said.

"This was none of your business." Mom slashed the air with one hand, face mottled red, shoulders so tight I was worried she might snap in half.

"Wrong." Sunny stepped forward, cold and beautiful. "This was every bit our business. Those vampires are our responsibility."

Mom drew a breath. "Fine, perhaps them." She glared

back and forth between them. "But you had no right dragging Syd into this mess with you."

"They are here because I asked them to come." I stared her down. Two could play this game. "They're right. This was every bit their situation to handle as it was ours."

I stressed *ours*. Hoped for a flicker of guilt from her.

Got one.

"We will take custody of the Wilhelm vampires now," Sunny said. "They will remain with us until our blood clan leader decides their fate."

Mom looked like she wanted to argue. The Council had, in fact, done just that, fought against the DeWinter clan's right to claim them. But Mom had to know Sunny and Frank took precedence.

"Fine," she snapped. "Get them away from my campus and out of my hair. I have enough problems."

Sunny nodded brusquely. "Trust me," she said, voice still chilly, "we have no desire to trouble you further."

She flickered into shadow and vanished, though Uncle Frank lingered. "You know, if it hadn't been for Syd, this whole thing could have turned into something much bigger. Something no one could handle."

"I was well aware of the situation," Mom said. Paused. "Not the details, no," she admitted. "But I had things under control. Then the pack of you," she pointed at Charlotte, Sassafras at my feet, and me, "had to run off like vigilantes and make a mess of things."

"We made a mess?" I shook my head, struggling to understand. "What?"

Ameline was the mess maker. I cleaned it up, thanks.

Correction. We.

Mom scowled at me so harshly I barely recognized her. "There are protocols here, Sydlynn," she snapped. "And Enforcers I employ to take care of such matters." She took a step back, one hand pressed to her forehead. "You could have been killed. Have you thought of that?"

"While you were compiling your facts and putting together your strategy," Sassafras snapped, "Ameline Benoit was gathering power. Enough power she almost succeeded in her goals this time. This time." He shook his furry head. "Honestly, Miriam."

Uncle Frank's handsome face darkened as he chopped one hand through the air, much like Mom had, as if cutting her off. "Don't bother trying, Sass," he said, voice full of bitterness. "Miriam's turned into a bureaucrat. She doesn't understand taking action any more. Or the meaning of thank you."

Before Mom could say anything, he, too, vanished.

Oh, stop it, Gram's voice cut in as Mom turned to me with her mouth open and clearly some strong words on her tongue. *Your girl saved your ass, daughter mine, and you know it.*

Stay out of this, Mother, Mom snapped.

I won't, Gram shot back. *Syd did everything right. Everything. She's a coven leader. You made her one. Time to treat her like she has a clue what she's doing.*

I was about to thank Gram when her attention spun on me. *And you*, she growled in a tight thread I knew only I could hear, *if you ever, ever, scare me like that again, I'll kill you myself.*

Now, Gram's power took the both of us and shook us a little. *Time to focus on what matters. Like that little bitch, Ameline, and what she has up her nasty sleeves next. Because you can bet she's not done.*

Not until she's dead, I sent.

Mom nodded sharply. *I know my duty, Mother.*

Do you? Gram sighed. *I wonder.*

I missed her when she was gone. Especially because I was now pretty much alone with Mom.

"You need to learn to let me handle these things." She wasn't about to back down on the issue, clearly. Which meant Gram was right. I had to show her I was capable.

But that would have to wait. If it ever happened. Likely she'd never really understand.

"What are you going to do about Ameline?" One thing was for sure, I had to keep the pressure on Mom. No going complacent. No Council committee to look into the matter. Ameline had to be tracked and put down like an animal.

I was happy to volunteer for the hunting party.

"I said leave that to me." Mom turned away from me. "You're threatening everything I've worked so hard to build the last several months." She turned back to me, but didn't look any happier, if less angry. "I'm trying to teach the covens working together is the best option. And then you run off when I had a group working on the issue. You pretty much proved to them you're dangerous."

"*I'm* dangerous?" I couldn't help the bark of laughter, and from the hiss and snarl I heard from Sassafras I wasn't the only one who had the same reaction. "You can't be serious."

"Think about it, Syd," she said. "You're not only part demon, you're Sidhe and now have the essence of all vampires living inside you. You're so powerful you can defeat a blood magic user." I almost protested and said it wasn't me until I realized she was right.

The vampire was me now.

Well, cool. Wasn't it?

"I'm already under immense pressure," Mom said. "I don't need one of my coven leaders turning into a Wild West cowboy whenever she feels the need for revenge."

Okay, I had to leave. Had to. Mom so didn't get it, didn't want to, I guess. Wasn't seeing things clearly. And if I didn't get the hell out of there, I was going to say and do some things from which our relationship might never recover.

"The Council, the other covens, can think what they want," I said, keeping my voice as cool and calm as I could. "But the law states I am a coven leader, autonomous. I obey the laws, Council Leader. I do my job. I protect my coven and the lives of the normals I interact with. Nothing I did was from revenge, but from my duty to protect my coven." I paused, a fist of stress in my stomach. "And I'm horrified you would ever think otherwise."

Mom's gasp told me I'd hit the mark, but when she called after me, her tone had changed completely.

"Syd." Soft. Almost kind. "Please, don't go like this. I'm sorry, sweetheart. I know you're doing your best."

My best. Wow. Great apology.

"Syd." Her hand settled on my shoulder. How she'd crossed the room so fast I had no idea, but I didn't unwind when she touched me. Her deep sigh did nothing for me either. "There's something we have to talk about."

"What?" What else? I didn't think I could take much more. Not from her. Not tonight.

This morning. Oh, hell.

"Quaid." Yeah, that conversation was going to happen. But what Mom said next wasn't what I was expecting. "I received a formal request from him. To join the Enforcers."

What remained of my heart was smothered in the chill of the only emotion I could muster as I swallowed my hurt and anger and grief in detachment.

"Thanks for letting me know."

I left, shrugging off her hand, sliding into the veil the moment I could.

41

I took the day off classes, spending it in my room, Charlotte in hers after I begged for some time alone. She seemed to understand and was less protective of me, I suppose because I'd faced down Ameline and won.

Mostly.

Why did it feel like a hollow victory? Maybe because Ameline was still out there. But worse than that, my whole life was a mess again. Alison was gone, turned into who knew what, now with the taste for blood driving her. And Quaid... an Enforcer. He'd chosen. I'd driven him away from me and he'd chosen to leave instead of fighting for us.

Typical.

I felt him on the other side of the door and almost didn't answer when he knocked, but knew I had to face him sometime. His deep brown eyes, so full of understanding and concern, almost did me in when I jerked the door open and caught his gaze.

"Syd." He lowered his hand from his attempt to knock. "I wanted to check on you. Make sure you were okay."

Contrite, wasn't he? Guess the whole looking for trouble thing had finally sunk in. And yet I couldn't bring myself to be angry with him, not anymore. I just felt tired all of a sudden, like I'd done everything I could even though I guessed I always knew it would never be enough.

I would never be enough.

"I should have been there for you." He didn't even ask to come inside. Told me volumes. "Not just about us, about love, about… when we…" Coward. Couldn't even talk about the night we spent together. "And not just about the attack last night. I'm never there for you." He sighed, broad shoulders sinking. "It seems like I'm always running, always hiding. Syd, I love you so much." I believed him, as much as I believed the but I knew was coming. "It's always been about disaster between us. Surviving it. Or making our own."

I nodded, leaning against the door jam. "I know, Quaid."

"I didn't want to believe you, the day you told me about Rupe and Simon." He shrugged a little. "I'd spent the whole summer finally being normal, you know? Being one of the group. For the first time ever. And when you brought up the possibility of trouble, I just couldn't go there."

Fair enough.

"Syd," he drew a breath, "I've made my choice."

"I know." I let the door swing against my foot, looking down at it, feeling the tap-tap-tap of the wood against my bare toes, focusing on that so I could say the next words I spoke without my voice shaking. "You chose the Enforcers."

"How did you…? Miriam." He let out a gust of air, hands jammed deep into his pockets.

"Yeah." I straightened.

"I just need to live for a while," he said. "No ties, no strings. No fate or destiny or geas from dead parents. No need for revenge, looking over my shoulder, second guessing what I'm doing because I'm dating a coven leader."

That zinged inside me. "So that's it."

He frowned, stiffening. "What's it?"

"The coven leader thing." It was so clear to me now, his fear, his distance. "It's too much for you."

Quaid didn't protest, didn't argue. "I just want my own life," he said. "I don't think it's too much to ask."

"Nope," I said, pushing back, ready to slam the door. "It's not. Have a nice one."

I felt him walk away from the other side of the still-vibrating door as I pressed my forehead to it, both palms flat against the wood as I waited for him to leave the building.

I couldn't stay in my room any longer. The air stifled me, made it hard to breathe. Likely the pressure in my chest came from another source, but I wasn't willing to consider it. I just needed to go outside in the sunlight and not think.

Charlotte followed me, but I ignored her, especially when she gave me lots of room and the privacy I desperately wanted. I found a bench, the same one I'd collapsed on before, beside the lovely little chapel, and sank to its surface, hugging myself tight and holding back the tears I knew would come if I let them.

It was over then. Between Quaid and I. He was going to be an Enforcer and I... a coven leader. And never the two shall meet. All the expectations I had, all the plans I'd made for us vanished in a puff of smoke. A half-laugh, half-sob choked me as I thought back to the first time I'd seen him, standing on my front step, so delicious—until I found out I was supposed to marry him.

It was like we'd been doomed from the start.

How could someone I loved so much—who I knew, I knew loved me too, just as much—walk away from what we had? And yet, I'd let him, hadn't I? I didn't exactly fight for us.

I gave him everything and he chose another life. And that was just the way things were.

The tears spilled, though I fought them as hard as I could. Blinded by them, I covered my face in my hands, swearing to myself this would be the last time I would cry over Quaid.

The very last.

And when strong arms encircled me, green Sidhe magic and the mixed scent of earth and fabric softener filled me, I clung to the one person who loved me unconditionally and wished things could be different.

Maybe I could learn to love Liam.

Maybe. But not yet. Not today. Today, I would cry and ache and let my heartbreak over Quaid out of me.

There was always tomorrow.

I settled into life at school pretty well after that. No more trouble. With no sign of Ameline or Rupe, things stayed that way. Even the Dumont brothers seemed more reserved, subdued, after Mom cleared them of wrongdoing when they claimed they knew nothing of Ameline's involvement in the Star Club.

Yeah, right. Still. Seeing them walk around campus with their heads down and nervous expressions did it for me.

As for the club itself, Mom saw to it the doors closed forever. When the older members involved were revived, drained of so much power they had to be fed from the Council magic, they didn't put up much of a fight, clearly shaken by their near death experiences. Still, I couldn't help but wonder if they would just trot off and start a new one all over again once the dust had settled.

Traditions and all that.

Sebastian contacted me the night after the attack to tell

me he was in negotiations with Yvette, the Matron of the Blood Clan Wilhelm, Sunny's old family. The following night he confessed he allowed Piotr and the others to go home, with the sworn blood oath they would never do anything like this again under threat of war.

Well… I trusted Sebastian. And it was his call.

I spent the next several weeks trying to help Simon adjust to school life again, but the vampire feedings and thrall had done so much damage even the healing witches who removed his memories were unable to restore him back to the person he was. Grades slipping, brilliant mind damaged, he disappeared from school without a word.

If for no other reason than the waste of my friend's potential, Ameline was going to die.

Painfully.

I'd had no word or touch from Alison, hardly surprising, though there were no reports of a demented blonde ghost drinking people's blood so there was hope she'd been unable to repeat the act.

The next time I saw Mia she was a shell of herself, all fake smiles and absent looks. It was clear she was weaker than ever, no sign at all she was taking action against the troublemakers in her coven or even paying much attention to her duties at all. When she vanished from school too, after my repeated requests to Mom to talk to her, I was hardly surprised.

But I was very, very worried.

It was weird seeing Quaid around campus, hanging out with his Enforcer friends, with the honey-blonde hanging from his arm openly now. I even caught them kissing one day, though they didn't see me, thankfully. Or the quick, horrible cry-fest I had behind one of the dorms before I could go back to class. So much for the pair of old codgers on the front porch swing. And for fate. Whatever destiny had been in store for me, it was now clearly altered by Quaid's needs.

Were all eighteen-year-old guys the same? I couldn't even begin to think Liam would have treated me the way Quaid did. So not fair to compare them, but really, really hard not to. One thing I did know for sure, as much I loved Quaid, I'd be thinking twice before trusting another guy with so much again, at least for a while.

Just wasn't worth the heartache without being absolutely sure. Next time? My terms.

Which made me think of Liam again.

Sigh.

Liam hadn't pressed the issue of his feelings and I was very grateful for that. I knew I'd have to do something eventually, but I just couldn't get past how I felt about Quaid and blamed it on the stupid magic I'd felt the night we'd spent together, though I told myself at least ten times a day I didn't love him anymore.

Liar.

And my sweet friend deserved better.

Worst though were Sunday dinners with Mom, all awkward and full of long silences Meira tried her best to fill. I finally stopped going all together, though I did make a point of spending as much time with my little sister as I could. When Mom wasn't around.

Which was all the time.

At least I had the distraction of working out the combination of my demon, Sidhe and vampire magic combined with the family power I controlled. The essence seemed eager to try new things, though she struggled with giving up herself to the others and I wondered if she'd ever fully integrate. She didn't fight me for control, at least, and since I proved myself worthy in her eyes, she seemed quite content to remain as part of the whole.

It was getting a little crowded in my head.

I didn't get to escape the poking and prodding, though thankfully the witches in charge of my examination kept things to a minimum. Probably because I'd managed to save their asses. At least someone appreciated what I'd done.

Mom accepted their final confused but satisfied report I wasn't a threat to anyone.

Could have saved them the effort.

Class was better, my teachers settling down now that the novelty of who I was had worn off. It took a few days after the Ameline mess before everyone started ignoring me again, but after that things were blissfully quiet.

Thanks in part to Sashenka and her friends, now mine. And Liam.

Always Liam.

Charlotte was giving me more space these days, but I found I didn't really want it and forced her to sit with us when I met with the girls. I even caught her laughing once.

Miracles do happen.

One major downside to my whole transformation was my acquired photosensitivity. All of a sudden I couldn't stand direct sunlight, my skin super touchy, dark sunglasses an absolute had to have. Thanks to the vampire inside me, I was slowly turning into a night owl.

Like I wasn't pale enough already. So much for my summer tanning sessions.

At least I had a firmer grip on my self-esteem by then.

I'd spent years doubting myself, hating what I was. Then worrying I was doing it wrong. But my days of wondering if I was good enough were gone. The only reason I felt like an outsider was because I chose to care what others thought. Funny, when I stopped, everything was different.

I kind of liked me, broken heart—mending—flaws and all. I'd survived so much, more than survived. I'd won. Any time my ego tried to drag me back down I remembered the look on Ameline's face when she began to crumble with age as we drained her of her power.

Yeah. I was good enough, damn it.

Time for a new attitude.

Like what you read? Find more at

pattilarsen.com

Now, try the first chapter of
Book Ten of the Hayle Coven Novels

PATTI LARSEN

AWARD WINNING YOUNG ADULT AUTHOR

FIRST PLANE

Snow slid down the back of my jacket, but I didn't care. I was having too much fun swishing my arms and legs back and forth while my little sister, Meira, did the same beside me. The sound of her giggling warmed me up enough the bit of a cold trickle down my neck sneaking past the collar of my coat and knit scarf didn't bother me so much.

I squinted up into the bright sunlight as Liam bent over me, mittened hands on his knees, a huge smile on his face. Green glints danced in his hazel eyes, blonde hair sticking out from under his hat.

I accepted his hand and let him pull me to my feet, turning to observe my handiwork. A perfectly—if I do say so myself—formed snow angel imprinted the crisp white of the park behind town hall, joined by a second as Liam leaned in sideways and practically scooped Meira up from the ground. The floppy red pom-pom on the top of her multi-colored toque bobbed to one side as she cast a critical eye over what she'd done.

"Mine's cuter," she said, bumping me with her shoulder and covering her mouth with her mittens, eyes sparkling.

"Mine's bigger." I shoved her back, sticking out my tongue while I pulled free one of my gloves and warmed my nose with my bare hand. "Big trumps cute."

"I don't know." Liam looked back and forth between them. "Cute is pretty awesome."

She beamed at him and hugged him while he winked at me, just as a giant, shaggy, black dog bounded toward us, his fur caked with blobs of white, and dove head first to our feet, completely obliterating the two angels.

"Galleytrot!" Meira stomped one foot as the eager hound of the Wild Hunt panted a huge grin at us.

"Meira!" He ducked his nose into the snow, flinging some at her, to which she squealed. "I love snow!"

"Yeah, hadn't noticed." I found myself laughing as he rolled over and over, grunting as he rubbed his back on the cold ground, tail thrashing, eyes flickering with red fire.

I turned to Liam, one hand in my jacket pocket. Yes. It was still there. My little gift, nice and safe, waiting for me to deliver it. Just as my fingers closed around it, Liam turned to me with a smile, bending over me, handsome face pink from the cold.

Before I could do or say anything, he hugged me, pressing

his cheek into my hair. I pulled free my gift, hugging him back, though I could feel my skin heat as Meira giggled again, a wicked look in her eyes, blue flashing to amber as she watched us.

I caught a glimpse of Charlotte over his shoulder, also watching, but my wereguard's normal flat expression told me nothing. Surprise, surprise. I'd been getting better at reading her lately, but I was already flustered enough having my little sister watch Liam hug me.

Don't get me wrong, he gave great hugs. But there was the little thing about him and his feelings for me while I, the idiot—yes, I admitted it—still couldn't bring myself to completely let go of Quaid. He'd dumped me, his choice, left me for the Enforcers and freedom, not wanting to be tied to a coven leader. But my heart, despite my resolve to let him go, didn't want to just yet.

And it was nowhere near fair to Liam to begin a relationship with him until it did.

Which meant we were friends, though the farce was hard to maintain at times, my guilt occasionally getting the better of me. Yet here I was, him showing his affection as usual.

At least I had something for him that would break the mood.

Boy, would it.

I slid my arms around his neck and dumped the perfectly formed snowball I'd been saving for him down the back of his shirt.

Cruel? Oh yeah. Funny? You freaking betcha.

Liam did the snow dance, laughing and howling all at the same time, jerking his shirt out of his pants under his bulky jacket, shaking it and himself until Meira and I were senseless in a hail of laughter. Even Charlotte smiled a little while Galleytrot snorted and shook his big head, snow pattering from his fur.

Liam turned at last, panting and flushed, eyes slits as he focused on me.

"You did *not*." It made me laugh harder he used one of my favorite expressions.

"I so *did*." I crossed my arms over my chest and smirked. "Come on then, Sidhe. Let's see what you've got."

Snowball fights rock. Especially when I win.

Finally worn out and ready to go inside for some hot chocolate, Meira, Charlotte and I left Liam and Galleytrot behind, the pair retreating with happy waves into town hall and the Sidhe cavern housing the Gate Liam guarded. My invite for them to join us was sweetly turned down, Liam eager to go back to his studying.

That boy. He needed to get his head out of books more often.

Thus the impromptu snow party. As we trudged back, I found myself smiling at the Christmas decorations gracing each house, the white lights wrapping each evergreen the town erected, waiting for dark so they could show off. I was happy to be home for break. As much as I really liked school and was having a great time now that the Star Club and their tainted connection to Ameline was disbanded, I missed being home.

There hadn't been any news from the former Dumont heir. I hadn't forgotten about her—hard to do when she almost killed me twice—but I had allowed Mom to lull me into a bit of a less paranoid state when she claimed she and the High Council weren't dropping the ball. Now leader of that Council, Mom had multiple Enforcers out looking for Ameline and I knew Mom was as determined as I to find the girl and bring her to justice.

The nice part was, even though things had been strained between Mom and I since the whole Ameline incident at the first of the semester, we'd both softened and let most of it go. Okay, not all of it. But enough we weren't snarking at each other every five seconds. And despite being super busy with her new duties and unavailable most of the time, Mom promise this Christmas week she'd be ours one hundred percent. No Council business.

Yeah, I'd believe that when it happened. Still, the alternative would have been my mother burned at the stake for allowing Dad to use blood magic in our house rather than taking the leader's seat on the Council, so I guess I could handle her being busy.

"Do you think Mom will like her present?" Meira was ten already, amazing. And growing like a weed. She stood to my shoulder and looked way more mature than most kids her age. The last six months had seen her demon features changing, as though she'd reached some milestone we didn't know about. It freaked me out a bit to see my little sister look like she was going on fourteen when she was still so young to me, but there wasn't much I could do about it. When she reached out with one hand and took mine, smiling at me, I still felt the girl inside her and that made it okay.

"I know she will." We didn't necessarily celebrate Christmas, per se. Not the religious form of it, anyway. But it had been a tradition in our family for as long as I could remember, Mom's attempt to make Meira and I feel like we were more like normal people, so present buying and stocking stuffing were still big parts of our celebration.

"Maybe we should get the other one." I smiled as Meira fretted over the pentagram necklace we'd chosen for Mom. She'd lost her favorite one over the summer and no amount of searching magic could uncover it. I knew it meant a lot to her, but it was Meira who suggested replacing it. We'd combed all the stores in Boston, finally narrowing our choices down to two.

"I like the one with the diamonds in it," I said. "You did too."

Meira bobbed a nod. "I know," she said. "But the other one was more traditional."

"We could have just made one, you know." I found myself laughing at her.

"I know," Meira said. "I just didn't think we could get it right."

Agreed. Neither of us was very good with metal. "We made the right choice. Those five diamonds were perfect to hold the different element fragments we embedded."

Meira grinned at me. "You're right," she sighed happily. "Now she can carry a bit of each of us around with her all the time." We'd both contributed a sliver of power, one for each gem.

"It was a great idea," I hugged her to me as we walked. "You're very thoughtful."

Her smile broadened before she startled me with her next question.

"Are you and Liam dating?"

Choke. "Um…"

She shrugged like it was no big deal. "I really like him," she said while Charlotte coughed softly behind me. Translation: Charlotte was laughing her fool noggin off inside her head.

Sigh.

Before I could offer my sister some clever answer that wouldn't say one way or the other, we both tensed. Not for a bad reason. Meira's little grin grew into wide-eyed excitement as she hopped up and down in the snow.

The rush of demon magic filled me with warmth as Dad crossed over.

Girls, he sent, rich mental voice touching us both. *I'm home.*

About the Author

Everything you need to know about me is in this one statement: I've wanted to be a writer since I was a little girl, and now I'm doing it. How cool is that, being able to follow your dream and make it reality? I've tried everything from university to college, graduating the second with a journalism diploma (I sucked at telling real stories), was in an all-girl improv troupe for five glorious years (if you've never tried it, I highly recommend making things up as you go along as often as possible). I've even been in a Celtic girl band (some of our stuff is on YouTube!) and was an independent film maker. My life has been one creative thing after another— all leading me here, to writing books for a living.

Now with multiple series in happy publication, I live on beautiful and magical Prince Edward Island (I know you've heard of *Anne of Green Gables*) with my very patient husband and six massive cats.

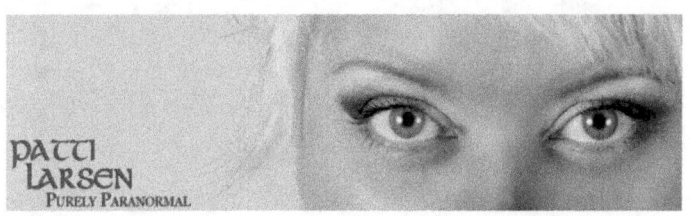

I love-love-love hearing from you! You can reach me (and I promise I'll message back) at **patti@pattilarsen.com**. And if you're eager for your next dose of Patti Larsen books (usually about one release a month) come join my mailing list! All the best up and coming, giveaways, contests and, of course, my observations on the world (aren't you just dying to know what I think about everything?) all in one place: **bit.ly/pattilarsenemail**

Last—but not least!—I hope you enjoyed what you read! Your happiness is my happiness. And I'd love to hear just what you thought. A review where you found this book would mean the world to me—reviews feed writers more than you will ever know. So, loved it (or not so much), your honest review would make my day. Thank you!

www.ingramcontent.com/pod-product-compliance
Lightning Source LLC
Chambersburg PA
CBHW060519180626
46817CB00002B/414